Born in San Francisco in 1955, Scott Bradfield is the author of *The History of Luminous Motion*, *What's Wrong With America*, *Animal Planet*, *Good Girl Wants it Bad*, and three collections of short stories, most recently *Hot Animal Love: Tales of Modern Romance*. He has written for film, radio, and television, and has lived in London since the mid-eighties. His stories, essays, and reviews have appeared most recently in *Bookforum*, *The New York Times Book Review*, *Poetry*, *The New York Ghost*, and *The Vintage Book of Contemporary American Short Stories*.

Praise for Scott Bradfield

"There is something in Bradfield's approach to the mystery of things that inevitably recalls the "Martian" poets or even the work of Nicholson Baker, although Bradfield is a sharper, deeper writer than these. He is always a joy to read, whether ironic and cutting as he surveys millenial chaos, or disturbing and disorienting in his intimations of mortality – individual and collective." —*New Statesman*

"Bradfield is a wild card, the Raymond Carver of the crystal-healing set." —*Independent*

"An inventive stylist who is leaving lots of tiny bite marks on T.C. Boyle's ankles. This puppy can howl." —*New York Times*

"Painfully beautiful writing." —**Mary Gaitskill**

"A wizardly writer of stories. His prose is so lucid and exact, his narrative sense so confident, that you hardly know where he's taking you until you're there." —**Tobias Wolff**

"Scott Bradfield has not simply staked out new literary terrain… he has mapped and colonized an entire new planet." —**Michael Chabon**

"This is the voice, recombinant and renewed, of Thomas Pynchon exploring the reaches of inner and outer space, Don DeLillo exposing the politics of technology, John Leonard spitting up the whole vile twentieth century… a daringly original literary sensibility…"
—*Newsday*

"Scott Bradfield's stories are ironic, funny, and at the same time filled with a haunting tension between the ordinary lives we lead and the darker dreams that lurk at the edge of our minds. He is the most original voice of the new generation of California writers."
—**Brian Moore**

Also by Scott Bradfield

1989: *The History of Luminous Motion* (novel)

1990: *Dream of the Wolf* (stories)

1993: *Dreaming Revolution: Transgression in the Development of American Romance* (criticism)

1994: *What's Wrong with America* (novel)

1995: *Animal Planet* (novel)

1996: *Greetings from Earth: New and Collected Stories*

2004: *Good Girl Wants It Bad* (novel)

2005: *Hot Animal Love: Tales of Modern Romance* (stories)

THE PEOPLE WHO
WATCHED HER PASS BY

A NOVEL
SCOTT BRADFIELD

TWO DOLLAR RADIO
Books too loud to ignore.

TWO DOLLAR RADIO is a family-run outfit founded in 2005 with the mission to reaffirm the cultural and artistic spirit of the publishing industry.

We aim to do this by presenting bold works of literary merit, each book, individually and collectively, providing a sonic progression that we believe to be too loud to ignore.

ISBN: 978-0-9820151-5-5
Library of Congress Control Number: 2010921758

Author photograph by Ji Li.
Designs and layout by Two Dollar Radio.
Typeset in Garamond, the best font ever.

TWO DOLLAR RADIO
Books too loud to ignore.
www.TwoDollarRadio.com
twodollar@TwoDollarRadio.com

For Ji

THE PEOPLE WHO
WATCHED HER PASS BY

GOODBYE LATELY

Late one night, when Salome Jensen was three years old, she was bundled up by the man who fixed the hot water heater and taken to live in a small, thinly furnished Van Nuys bungalow apartment. She knew it was wrong and too abrupt for a proper holiday, and that the man, who insisted she call him Daddy, wasn't her real daddy. But from the moment she was deposited into the back of his warm, garlic-scented Volkswagen-van, she knew she was safe and secure from all the things her parents had kept her safe and secure from until now. She didn't cry, she didn't resist, and she knew that everything would turn out, as Mommy liked to say, "for the best." Eventually, she even learned to accept their life together as a sort of home.

"I'm not saying I can ever replace your real mommy and daddy," the man told her that night while she drifted in and out of consciousness in back of his van. "And I know there's all sorts of reasons you'll remember your genetic parents as important figures in your life, as well you should. But at the same time, I care for you very much in my own special way, and not in any of those sick, perverted ways you hear about in tabloid television programs and newspapers. I care about you as a perfect, beautiful little child with a fresh perspective on this sorry world of ours. And it's precisely this sort of fresh perspective which may yet save us all from total eco-catastrophe and self-annihilation."

She never knew his real name before the night she called him

Daddy. He had always simply been the man who fixed the hot water heater. Then, suddenly, he was a lot more.

"I need my bunny," she told him. She had wrapped herself in an oily, perforated pink blanket she found on the corrugated steel floor of the van. It smelled like rusty water. "And my Cadbury Creme Egg."

He was a very distant, contemplative sort of man, not given to the sudden rough and tumble horsey-rides and hide-and-seeks of her original, now-obsolete and nearly-forgotten daddy. Whenever he responded to something she said, it took her by surprise, as if they were sharing something more intimate than a place to sit, or a car for taking you places.

"There are lots of things you think you need in this world," he told her, speaking from deep inside the far-off, rock-hard certainty of himself. "And lots of things you don't need at all. Once you learn the difference, sweetheart, I'll have accomplished everything I set out to accomplish on the day I became your devoted and lifetime daddy."

He sacrificed everything for her, including the tiny back bedroom of their bungalow apartment, which he painted pink and blue with white cloud-like bunnies on the walls and ceiling. He sold the tools from his van to buy her a bed with a flouncy, bunny-imprinted duvet and matching fitted sheets. He bought her a plastic telephone, a plastic washer-dryer, and a matching Home Cooking Play Corner, which interrupted the pale stucco walls like a random glimpse into another world. Most mornings, while Daddy was still in the shower, Sal stood at the Home Cooking Play Corner and mixed together tidy round containers of flour, salt, and Play-Doh in a large Pyrex mixing bowl with a plastic whisk. The mixing bowl had been left behind by previous tenants in one of the high over-painted wooden cabinets alongside a water-stained box of Blue Point matches, a tapeworm-like yellow flea collar scribbled with blond dog hairs, and a petrified sponge.

"Most of this stuff is useless," Daddy told her when he climbed down from the draining board. "But this Pyrex bowl and sponge are perfectly okay. And there's no point spending any money we don't have to."

He slept every night on the living room sofa, filling up a large Quaker Oats Oatmeal tin with Salem cigarette butts and Heath Bar candy wrappers. And in the morning, when Salome went to wake him, a thick gray mist hung from the fissured ceiling like the gauzy, fly-entangled draperies that adorned the garage windows in Salome's other, more distant home, the one she didn't like to think about anymore. Sometimes, the peat-like butts and ashes of the Oatmeal tin were still smoldering when Salome woke, and when she couldn't extinguish the buried sparks with a rubber pencil-eraser, or the butt of a plastic bottle, she poured in the pulpy residue from Daddy's last can of V8 juice and, with a folded newspaper or magazine, manufactured thick, periodic pulses of smoke, like Indian signals in an old movie, as if somewhere in the back of her mind she was trying to communicate something to someone about something that had happened a long time ago.

A place she had been, perhaps. Or a person she had met while she was there.

Some mornings Salome awoke to the sound of Daddy whistling in the bathroom, where the shower made a hollow, reverberative sound against the loose drain-board, like sand being blown across an aluminum rooftop.

The first time she knocked, he didn't reply. So she stood her ground, took a deep breath, and knocked again.

"I need to pee," she whispered. He probably couldn't hear over the noise of the shower. "Every morning when I wake up," she explained, "I need to go to the bathroom."

Behind the gray plastic shower curtain, Daddy's body produced a jagged, almost colorless lump of shadow, like something at the bottom of a muddy pond.

"What's that, sunshine? I'll be out shortly! Fix yourself something to eat in the kitchen! I won't be long now!"

Outside their bungalow apartment, the cracked driveways and gardens were overgrown with tall yellow weeds. If you weren't careful, they scratched the insides of your legs when you squatted, and the scratches continued stinging long after breakfast. In Daddy's house, "breakfast" meant a big dry bowl of Lucky Charms cereal, a banana, and a glass of V8.

V8 juice was the only store-bought beverage Daddy allowed in the house. And while Salome could live without it, Daddy claimed that she was lucky to get as much V8 juice as she did.

"Some daddies," he explained, showing her the red and white tin can as if it were a devotional candle in an empty church, "don't allow any decent-tasting beverages in the house whatsoever. You get boiled tap-water three times a day, or a can of orange soda. You never get anything that replenishes your natural juices *and* tastes good. It's all one or the other in most people's houses, but in *my* house, I believe in doing what comes natural. Even if it means placing myself at odds with the rest of this crazy, hyper-repressive country called America."

Salome didn't like disagreeing, so she finished her V8 juice and kept quiet. She had never upset Daddy during their time together, and she didn't want to start now. After all, he might be the last decent daddy she ever had.

And if there was one thing that Salome had learned, it was that a girl needed to hold on to what she possessed in this world. Or she might lose it all over again.

———

Many things didn't happen at Daddy's house. They didn't go to play group, for example. They didn't go swimming, or to movies, or to Music School at the new mall. They didn't even have friends over, or visit friends in other houses. Most of the time, they just sat inside the bungalow apartment, trying to find ways to deter the hot valley sun by folding musty cardboard boxes into the embrasures of blistering window frames, or hanging curtains of aluminum foil over the doorways. Then, after what he liked to call a "job well done," Daddy would lie on the scratchy osier sofa, smoke, and stare at the broken television, a large sentry-like Panasonic with a kidney-shaped stain on the screen, and Sal would return to the plump, clean bed in her bedroom and gaze at her Home Cooking Play Corner, feeling the same distant introspection that Daddy seemed to feel whenever he told her things.

"Why don't you fix Daddy something to eat!" Daddy shouted from the other room. "Maybe an omelet, or scrambled eggs. And lots of hot coffee. Bring me a pot of hot coffee and don't stop brewing till I say so." During the day, Daddy wore a green terrycloth bath-towel secured around his waist with a safety-pin, which permitted him to scratch the fine black hairs on his belly.

An omelet, Sal thought. Scrambled eggs. She observed the neat plastic oven and cabinets. She looked out the dust-stained window at dead weeds in the yard, and the abandoned hulks of ominously silent fridge-freezers. Inside Daddy's house, pink bunnies adorned the walls. And a thick green feathery parrot had been painted on her wooden headboard. Daddy spent three days encouraging her to call the headboard Polly, but Sal could only think of it as The Green Entity.

"I don't have any eggs or butter," she said softly. "I only have flour and salt."

"You could bake cakes!" Daddy shouted. The softer Sal spoke, the louder Daddy did. "You could bake bread and cookies!"

It was hard to explain things to Daddy. He could do things with his hands, such as hammer pieces of wood together, or hang pictures on the wall, but he couldn't imagine other people doing them; his organism didn't work that way.

"I'd need a real oven to bake bread," she said, so soft she could hardly hear herself. You had to sneak out the back door of a conversation with Daddy, or else he might follow you around for hours, leaving you no time to figure things out for yourself. "You can't bake bread in a plastic oven, Daddy. The whole thing would melt all over the floor."

Every night, he sat on the edge of her bed until he thought she was asleep, stroking the bunnies imprinted on the foot of her duvet and aimlessly telling stories of the strange and distorted life he had lived before becoming Daddy.

"When I was a little boy, I possessed no sense of permanence or location," he told her. "I was always moving from one military base to another, one school to another, one set of bully-boys who wouldn't play with me to another set of bully-boys who wouldn't play with me either. As a result of these constant dispossessions, I developed a very private sense of what's important in life, and this importance, as you might expect, is not attached to things of a material nature. It's not an issue of what car somebody drives, or whether they saw the latest cool movie or not. Rather, true happiness and fulfillment is a place that's always inside you, no matter where you're located on some stupid map. My daddy was what you might call a hard man, Sal. He never hit me, but he never showed me much affection either. Some days, he made me clean the patio with a toothbrush; other days, I had to sleep on the patio in my underpants without a blanket, which was a lesson designed to teach me hardness. Now I may not agree with the way my daddy taught me these lessons, Sal – and I promise I'll never be the sort of daddy who asks you to clean the patio with a toothbrush – but I do agree with the *lessons* he taught me, and the most important lesson was this: In order to endure the meaningless rituals of this world, one must develop a hardness to material conditions. Listen to the part of yourself that is resistant to conditions, Sal, and you will live a perfect life. One where you always remain true to yourself."

His stroking of the bed was steady, long, and fearful of actual contact with Sal. If his fingers snagged her toe or kneecap, even momentarily, he flinched and drew back, as if stung by an electrical charge. With every stroke of his hand, he subsided into his own body, as if he were drifting off on a glassy lake far away, maybe Switzerland or Brazil. Sal always wondered where he went when he drifted away like that; she hoped that next time he might take her with him. She would hate to be left behind in this too-big bed all alone.

Every morning, while Daddy cleansed himself in the bathroom, Salome ventured into the cool, discrete shell of his white Volkswagen van and examined the merchandise he had brought home the night before. Some daddies worked in offices, and some worked in construction, but Salome's daddy loaded and unloaded things in the night, transporting them home to this driveway where only Salome could touch them. Black oily car batteries leaking a streaky yellow matter. Sheets of metal and plyboard, collapsed cardboard boxes, and broken Styrofoam packing materials. Cardboard promotional displays of large, short-skirted women holding prominent cans of beer and soda pop; heavy chunks of machinery with moving parts and sticky surfaces. Flanges, rotors, switches, plugs, and sockets. You could articulate these objects with one another, and teach them to operate as a single unit. This piece tells this piece to open, Sal thought. This piece tells this piece to shut. Some mornings, she attached the thick rust-embossed parts to one another until they resembled something breathing underwater. A creature with bolts for eyes, electrical cords for tentacles, and a big crooked mouth filled with knobby bolts for teeth. How unusual to find you down here, the nodding creature seemed to say when Sal picked it up from the dead ocean floor. A pretty little girl in a clean pink dress.

It was cool down here in the Great Rift, Sal thought. The world moved slowly, and nobody worked very hard. Perhaps it was because the planet generated a thin current of energy. You could be alone down here for hours and not even notice time go by. It was the perfect place for a man like Daddy.

Sometimes, though, Sal encountered another voice down in the Great Rift, amongst the gnarled electrical devices and loosely strewn flywheels and crumbling rubber floormats. It flicked and flitted in every direction, like a school of darting, microscopic fish.

"Should you be playing with those, little girl? They're awfully dirty. Shouldn't you be in school, or watching TV? Where did you find those filthy things anyway? Does your daddy know you're out here? Why don't you put those things away and play with something decent, like dollies or plastic teacups?"

Sal could always tell when the landlady was nearby. Hard little sparks of movement popped around her, as if she were cloaked by a haze of static electricity.

"What about my glasses, little girl? Have you seen my glasses anywhere? I can see perfectly fine without my glasses, but I need them to read the paper. What sort of work does your daddy do anyway? Would you like to tell me about your daddy, or would you rather help me find my glasses? Then we can go back to my place and wash those filthy hands. If you were my little girl, I wouldn't let you get so dirty. I'd wash you really good in the morning, and you'd have to stay clean all day."

Her name was Mrs Anderson, and she wore a thick padded blue housecoat, glasses adorned with butterflies, and a large sun-stained, chipped lapel pin that declared:

Olympics in '84!

Whenever she came up to the van's dusty, oil-smeared window, she cocked her head, peering out of one glaucoma-ridden eye like a fish in a bowl.

Mrs Anderson's questions were never easy to answer. But then, as Salome was beginning to realize, that was true about most questions.

"I don't know," Salome said simply, trying to keep her responses accurate, clean, and totally unrevealing. She had learned to clamp the rubbery black polyps of plastic spark plug attachments to her arms and wrists. The suction cups left red spots on her skin, like measles. "I think Daddy's self-employed. He never tells me what he does. And I never saw your glasses. But if I do see them, I promise to let you know."

Mrs Anderson was the only person Sal had ever met who smoked as much as Daddy – long skinny cigarettes imprinted with flowers and curlicues.

"Put that down," Mrs Anderson barked between puffs. "You could electrocute yourself with that. So where's your daddy now, little girl? Does he like to sleep late? Every halfway decent man I ever knew liked to sleep late, it's like living with the dead. Is your daddy married? Has he got a partner of any kind? Maybe I should come over and visit. We always have trouble with the hot water in Bungalow 7. I should probably come over, check the hot water, and maybe look for my glasses while I'm at it."

Salome remained firm in back of the van. She wasn't going anywhere Daddy didn't take her.

"I don't know," she said, a little surprised by her answer. "I don't think he's married. I'm not really sure."

You couldn't startle a woman like Mrs Anderson. She always knew exactly what she wanted to say.

"You need a permanent life-long partner if you're going to survive past forty, little girl. But until you turn forty, you should enjoy yourself with as many boys as possible. Me, I lost my main partner to drugs, being he was a mean man with no sense of moderation. Has your daddy got a sense of moderation, little girl? Or has he always been more the excessive-type personality to you?"

Salome pretended to think for a moment. She didn't want to leave too quickly. A woman like Mrs Anderson would follow a person like Sal around until she took everything. Sort of like the dogs who hung around tables at meal times.

"I don't know," Sal said, applying more of the black rubbery polyps to her arms. "I guess that depends on what you mean by moderation."

That night, great gusts of rain sprayed the doors and windows of Bungalow 7, stirring up brief gray vortices of shells and gravel and rolling around the garden like huge dark bowling balls.

"Once a woman like Mrs Anderson catches whiff of a man like me," Daddy said over a dinner of scrambled eggs and fish sticks, "she won't stop until she's vacuumed up every crumb of his being and mopped up every drop of his blood. The moment he opens his eyes, she'll already be there, peering at his forehead through those thick bifocal glasses she's always losing. What's that little black dot? she'll ask, picking at his forehead with one of her gray thorny fingers. Is that a mole? Did you ever get that checked? Do you use conditioner on that scalp? Have you ever heard of moisturizer? Every possible fact there is to know about you she'll need to know yesterday. Like how many jobs you've had, or where you got that funny scar on your elbow. Your Social

Security number, car registration, who you voted for in the last election, it's all catnip to these chicks. I've met a lot of girls like Mrs Anderson in my life, sunshine, and they can't be happy in their solitary nature. They devote every waking minute to seeking out strong, character-driven men like myself, trying to hook us up to the old ball and chain. We aren't individuals to women like that, sunshine. We're producers of profit and fat. We're only on this earth to fix their hinges, or pay their bills. And so far as our own personal happiness is concerned, well, that's no concern of theirs at all. We're just extensions of *them*. We're just here to do whatever it is they can't do for themselves."

Salome could feel the storm reverberate in the thin, slanted wooden table with her fingertips, as if she were engaged in a séance with weather. She liked fish sticks with ketchup, but Daddy didn't allow ketchup in his house. He said that ketchup, like many things you could buy at the supermarket, took all the proper joy out of a nice cold glass of V8.

"It's like we try to find our way in a world that doesn't want us," Daddy said, gazing off at the fluttering sheets of aluminum foil hanging from the window. "We try to stay together, but the world just tears us apart. It makes me wonder sometimes, sweetheart, why anybody would ever make the effort to be a good daddy in such a crazy world, or to raise his daughter the best way he knows how. In the long run, nothing lasts, not even childhood. When you get right down to it, children are probably the least dependable creatures there are."

That night, Sal lay awake and listened to water running outside in the streets, splashing against itself in loose little eddies and counter-eddies, trying to find a place it hadn't been. But the world was too wet for water; there wasn't anywhere left for it to go. Cars ripped through the streets; headlights flared in the windows, and something nebulous and half formed slowly made its way across the night.

It might be an owl, she thought. A wolf, an alligator, or a fox. Or it might be another daddy in another van, with a lot of different, un-Daddy-like notions about what to eat and what to wear. Perhaps there wasn't room for all these daddies banging around out there, looking for places they hadn't been, or children they had never known. In some ways, maybe daddies were like water. Always on their way to somewhere else, forming shapes and losing them, dripping like clocks in secret caverns that you couldn't see. If they stayed in the same place too long, or assumed the same shape, they'd be found by the forces that looked for them. They'd be devoured and transformed into someone different than who they were supposed to be.

"Little girl? Hello? Are you safe in there? Will you let me in? I heard your daddy drive off and thought you might be frightened. Do you want to come stay with Mrs Anderson until your daddy gets back? Are your electricals working properly? How about the plumbing and running water? Have you people even got a phone? How can people live in a house like that without a telephone? I'm telling you, little girl, I don't understand men whatsoever. They don't have any idea how to raise a little girl at all."

Then, like celestial punctuation, the vast inarticulate storm struck the roof with a huge, tree-muffled fist, causing the curtains to billow and the floors to crack. Even the aluminum sheets on the windows chimed faintly, and something fugitively hissed. A water heater or a pipe.

"Little girl! I'm letting myself in with my key! Is there water on the floor? The last time it rained this hard there was water all over the floor! I'm not trying to be nosy, little girl! I just got to make sure those new floors of mine aren't covered with water!"

If you waited long enough, it would take you away. It would not look twice at the bunnies, or the blankets, or the Home Cooking Play Corner, or at any of the things you had established to make this fragile space seem permanent.

It would simply wrap you in its arms and hold you tight. It would teach you all the secrets you weren't supposed to know.

———

"Men run away from love; it's in their nature," Mrs Anderson told Sal the next morning. They were sitting in a cheery blue breakfast nook eating eggs, bacon, and cottage cheese. The walls were adorned with little plastic models of Jesus dying on the cross, glass-framed butterflies, and faded photographs of ugly children scowling into a camera. "They see love come their way and they head for the hills, it's some instinctual reaction they're born with. Men're basically lone wolves, little girl, wandering around in their big white Volkswagen vans, and running like hell at the first sign of trouble." Mrs Anderson wore a big plastic blue bubble on her head, knobby with hair curlers. She smoked lengthy cigarettes and crushed them out in her half-finished fried eggs with brisk little movements, as if she were extinguishing each man she had ever known, one mistake at a time.

"Trust me, little girl. I've had five men take off on me in the last twelve years, and they were as different as five different species of animal. But they were all identical in one respect, and that was their fear of love, commitment, and marital harmony. When I *didn't* love them, boy, there wasn't no problem; we got along great. In fact, when I *didn't* love them, they hung around forever, there was no place they'd rather be than with their hot-looking little yours truly. They fixed broken boards on the roof. They repaired plumbing and electrical problems. For a while, I'd have everything a woman wanted: sex in the afternoon, home-delivered pizzas and cigarettes, and a competent man to lay carpets and hang drapes. He'd be halfway polite and considerate, even decent-looking, until I started developing this affection. I'd try to suppress it, but it'd just well up somehow, like this natural mineral spring all women possess, the healing spiritual power of all feminine nature. Which is when they'd get jittery, and the more jittery they got, the more I started feeling affection, like they were this planetary force just pulling me down to destruction. Eventually, I couldn't live without them. I wanted to hold them all the time and cook their favorite meals. I'd wake in the night to check if they were breathing, it got terribly obsessive. Finally, after being abandoned by so many men I can't remember their names, there was this one boy – a man, really – named Roy Hattersfield, who completely screwed me up. I loved Roy Hattersfield so much that I started checking if he was breathing within a few days of the first time we slept together. I even took medication to control it, but I couldn't stop. I'd wait until late at night; I'd hear him falling asleep, and right away I'd start listening for his raspy breath, in and out, in and out, until the breathing would subside and eventually disappear, especially if he slept on his back. Then I'd go to the bathroom and get this little hand-held mirror I used for shaving my legs, and hold it up to his nose. If he was breathing, he'd leave this moist little streak of breath on the glass. It was like this whiff of spirit he emanated through his nose. It looked so delicate and fine, almost like a drop of sugar water, and sometimes I'd be tempted, I just couldn't help myself, and I'd lean forward and taste it with my tongue. It tasted like the coolest water imaginable. I always thought spirit would be warm and tangy, but it isn't. It's more like cool and sweet. I ran it around on my lips with my tongue, and felt that spirit coming into my body, and suddenly I felt this affection growing inside me again, the one I wasn't supposed to feel, even more powerful than a baby inside you. Believe me, little girl, I've experienced both types of fullness in my life, and this one is better. Sometimes, I'd be staring at him so intensely, he'd just suddenly open his eyes and see me holding that mirror, and maybe tasting his spirit with my tongue, like I was being suggestive of carnal intercourse, but being suggestive was the furthest thing from my mind. Then, one night, completely by surprise, Roy Hattersfield – if that *was* his real name – shot up in bed so fast I almost dropped my mirror, and stared at me like I was crazy. After that, things went seriously wrong with our relationship – not to mention something went seriously wrong with Roy Hattersfield. He stopped touching me, and loving me, and helping me polyfill cracks in Bungalow 12. When a relationship breaks down, little girl, it's always the female who feels guilty, even though there's nothing she can do about it. At that point, I had two children to raise, and they were getting into everything. I couldn't just go running after Roy Hattersfield, no matter how much I wanted him back. That would be a really mature piece of behavior, leaving my kids alone with the Liquid Plumber and the silverware cleanser to chase after some man like Roy Hattersfield. Especially when Roy Hattersfield wasn't even their real daddy."

Daddy's impression was already disappearing from the flooded interior of Bungalow 7, where green water lay in thick glossy sheets across the wooden floors and carpets like the protective plastic tarp draped over a baseball diamond. When hazy sunlight through the window caught the skin of water just right, it flashed off floating bedbugs and carpet mites, cigarette butts and gray leaves that swirled in a slow chiaroscuro, like galaxies of stars and raw matter. When they went over the next morning, Sal wasn't sure what they were looking for. She was confused by the paradoxical (and not entirely unattractive) concept that Mrs Anderson kept referring to as "Sal's things."

"Don't you have any toys or any books, little girl? What about dolls? Where's your favorite dolly? God, this place smells. Did your daddy ever clean the toilet? What's growing in there, anyway? I've never seen a plant growing out of anybody's toilet before. Maybe it's just as well your daddy headed for the hills. I'm not one of these neatness freaks you hear about, but I draw the line at plants in the toilet. You wouldn't believe what root systems like that do to the plumbing. And finding a decent plumber who knows how to deal with them? Totally impossible. Now look, what's that in there? That looks like a really nice toy for a girl your age. It sure doesn't look like your daddy's. Somehow, I don't see your crazy daddy baking pretend cookies and pies."

Oven. Stove. Dishwasher. Leaning at strange angles in three inches of green water. Clogged with memories and debris like the plant in the toilet.

Sometimes they didn't know and you had to tell them.

"It's my Home Cooking Play Corner," she told Mrs Anderson. "But I don't feel like cooking anymore. We might as well leave it here."

Living with Mrs Anderson was the same only different. You woke together, ate breakfast together, went shopping together, and watched television together, as if you were attached at the hip by a short tight filament of skin. Even when you peed, Mrs Anderson accompanied you, sitting on the edge of her gleaming, immaculate white bathtub, and pulling back the shower curtains to provide room for her gesturing. Mrs Anderson wasn't as secretive as Daddy. She always had something to say, and she didn't care who heard it.

"The last thing we should do, little girl, is contact the child welfare people, with whom I've had my share of personal experience over the years, believe you me. These child welfare people start showing up with their clipboards and splattered ink blots and you don't know what they're asking. Did you touch your baby, did your baby cry in the night, did you use drugs in front of your baby, do you ever wake in the night worrying about your baby, what sort of psychotic baby-abuser are you, anyway? Jesus Rice Crispies. It's like all they do is sit around thinking up new ways to harm babies and wondering if you subscribe to them. Did you ever harm your baby physically? Did you ever harm your baby psychologically? Of course I goddamn did, I'm a mom, and that's one of the things that happens with a baby. You drop them and pick them up again. You lose them in the supermarket and find them. You burn them on the stove when you're cooking, and prick them with a needle while sewing on buttons. It's a goddamn baby, for Christ's sake; it's not made to last forever. And so far as those bruises, the damn thing fell over and bumped its head, that's what babies *do*! But do they listen? Of course they don't. Now please take your fucking clipboards out of here and leave me alone!"

Mrs Anderson often started yelling at the drop of a hat. Afterwards, she subsided and grew contemplative, her glasses foggy and opaque.

"So," she sighed, "if you think for one minute I'm going to let those child welfare people into *this* house again, you've got another thing coming. I've already lost two kids to those people. I'm not planning to lose another."

Salome sat on the toilet and held her bony knees together, recalling the big oily patch in the driveway where Daddy's white van had been. There was something very comforting about that stain; it felt like the spaces under a familiar bed, where you could hide safely from the world and only be found again when you were ready. Her perforated, oil-stained wool blanket, crumpled in the back seat of the white van, was probably fulfilling a similar purpose for Daddy right now. It marked a space in the world that contained nothing at all.

"What are you doing, little girl? Didn't your father ever teach you how to wipe yourself? Here, take this."

Mrs Anderson briskly folded three squares of toilet paper together like the leaves of an urgent letter.

"There you go. Three sheets are plenty. And when you're finished, flush that toilet all the way. I don't want weeds sprouting out of it like at your daddy's. Then pull up your pants and get in the car. I need cigarettes at the market, eggs, bacon, and a halfway decent *TV Guide*."

———

By now, Sal could see it coming a million miles away.

"You've got no drainage," explained the man who arrived in a large green truck that said Dave's Drainage and Hauling on the side. "And your water table's completely out of whack. Who told you to build a house on a water table like that? He must've been totally nuts."

Mrs Anderson was wearing her brand new padded blue housecoat. She leaned her face into the man's view whenever he tried to look away. Earlier that day, they had driven to Sears in Burbank and purchased the new housecoat along with some bright pink nail polish, pink lipstick, and a pair of fuzzy blue slippers.

But the man who drove the truck wasn't too concerned with Mrs Anderson's housecoat or her flashing pink nails. Instead, he directed the course of his monologue directly at Salome, who was wearing a large water-stained smock chopped down to size from one of Daddy's abandoned, over-washed gray Pendleton sport-shirts.

"Which means we'll need to suck it out of the house with my generator, and dig you a septic tank, and arrange some proper drainage for this wobbly water table you've got. I can't give you an estimate till I start digging. Sometimes it's just sand down there, but sometimes it's solid. And if it's solid rock, boy, look out. That rock can run into money."

The weeds had been flattened into a vast, soggy mass of burrs and gray, pulpy stems. When Salome looked around, she saw three bungalow apartments, arranged in a semi-circle like wagons at an Indian attack. In two windows, elderly Latin women stood blinking against their own reflections. It was as if they lived in a different world than Salome's, where nobody could see or hear them. They could hardly see or hear themselves.

"That's a cute little girl you got," the man who drove Dave's truck told Salome. "And unlike most cute little girls, she's extremely well behaved."

It was at this moment that Salome saw the sunflower. It was standing on the far side of the compound, a huge porous yellow face, lashed by green leaves. It was trying to catch her attention.

"She has her bad points," Mrs Anderson told the man who drove the truck. She was still showing him her new housecoat, flirting the right lapel back and forth at him, as if wiggling a TV antenna for better reception. "She hardly says anything, and she eats like a pig. You wouldn't believe how much she eats. It's like having this big black bottomless pit in the house, and it's located right next to the fridge."

Salome could feel the man's eyes staring into her back as she walked across the yard to examine the tall leaning sunflower. The sunflower was in a stern and reproachful mood. It wanted to know what Salome was doing staring like that, and thinking these thoughts she just couldn't stop thinking.

"Well," the man said, "I guess you got no choice but to feed them. Or else those goddamn child welfare people get wind of things. And before those clowns are finished, you won't remember the kid's name or what she looks like. I've dealt with my share of child-welfare people, lady, and believe me. I know whereof I speak."

The man who drove Dave's truck couldn't believe all the rock he encountered, or how hard it was draining Bungalow 7. "I'll be back tomorrow," he said, one day after another, recoiling his long corrugated hoses from the yard where they had lain all day like the tentacles of some collapsed mechanical octopus. "I can't believe how much these old septic tanks interfere with the runoff. And I already mentioned the water table. The water table in this part of the world is totally shot."

He returned the next morning, and the morning after that. Unspooled gray plastic tentacles across the yard and inserted their dribbling mouths through the doors of the flooded bungalows. Pretty soon, the drainage pump was chugging and smoking like a factory while the man sat alone in his truck, drinking beers, eating packaged sandwiches, and listening to all-talk sports stations on the dashboard radio.

Sal tried to be careful when she ventured outside. If the man saw her before she saw him, it felt like betrayal.

"Come keep me company, little girl," the man said. "Do you want to sit with me and help run the generator?"

Sal wasn't being difficult. She just thought she should stay out of everybody's way.

"That sunflower doesn't have any of these delicious barbecue-flavored potato chips, little girl. Do you want some of my barbecue-flavored potato chips? They're really tasty, and nowhere near so bad for you as lots of junk-food I could name."

Barbecue-flavored potato chips were Sal's favorite type of potato chips in the entire world.

"You seem lonely with nobody to play with, little girl. When I was little, I was never so lonely as you. I had friends all over the neighborhood, we were always cooking up something. Sports clubs, baseball, bowling. Killing things with a spyglass, or sneaking into people's houses. You want to know the funniest thing about sneaking into people's houses, kid? It doesn't feel funny at all. It's almost like you belong there, even when you're hiding behind the couch and they come home and don't see you. It's almost like they know you're there and they're playing along. Nothing bad can happen to you. You just feel really safe and warm."

The sunflower was beginning to sag, concerned about all this water that wouldn't go away. Salome had tried propping it up with sheets of cardboard, sticks, coat hangers, anything she could find, but you couldn't slow some things down. The sunflower had learned too much. It was tired of knowing. One of its brown arms was falling off, like the sleeve of an old coat. The porous yellow face was spotty with caterpillars.

"That man's trying to be nice to you," Mrs Anderson told Sal one day, in an ominous voice that fulfilled all of Sal's expectations. Mrs Anderson was wearing lipstick, rouge, and eyeliner, like one of those cracked, half-sentient dolls staring up at you from wooden tables in neighborhood garage sales and basement thrift shops. "You shouldn't ignore him, little girl. You should be nice back. He wants to know about us. He's indulging his natural God-given curiosity. Tell him I'm divorced, no, single, no, my husband died in the war. Tell him I own all these properties and I'm thinking about making a will, all I need's a good lawyer. And while we're at it, let's not mention your daddy for a while. We wouldn't want things to get too complicated and scare this nice man away."

As the sunflower grew smaller in the flooded yard, kneeling into itself like a broken kite, Salome delivered hot soups and thermoses of coffee to the man in the truck, who always brushed a clear space in the breadcrumbs and newspapers so she could sit beside him in the sun-split and cigarette-charred vinyl seat. He even let her play with the dashboard's large green knobs and switches, cranking levers back and forth, turning dials, and pushing the large chrome buttons that didn't seem connected to anything. They activated nothing but themselves.

When the man finished eating, arrayed in a fresh blanket of crumbs, he told her about himself. Whether she asked him to or not.

"I used to have a lovely little girl like you," he said. "She had blonde hair like you, and natural curls like you, and big fat eyelashes like you. And even though her mommy and I weren't married, she always called me daddy, and let me give her horsey rides, and take her to the park."

At this point, like a magician, he would show Salome a barbecue-flavored potato chip, turn it over in one direction, and then in the other. This is a perfectly intact little potato chip, he seemed to be saying. Just like you.

"Would you like a horsey ride, little girl?" the man said finally, and placed the tongue-sized potato chip in his mouth, crunching it with a slow, methodical pulse of his jaw. "Would you like me to take you to the park and give you a ride on the swings?"

Salome looked out the dirty window at the slowly deflating sunflower. Then she looked at the front door of Mrs Anderson's house. Mrs Anderson, emblazoned with cosmetics like some-body on a poorly tuned color TV, was making urgent motions with her hands. "Go on!" her urgent hands told Salome, as if they were shooing flies towards a sheet of flypaper. "Get on with it! We don't have all day!"

Salome pretended to think about this for a while. Then she said, "I've already been to the park today. And I don't feel like a horsey ride at this exact moment."

On the other hand, the sunflower did the opposite of beckoning. Folding into itself. Saying goodbye to the life that was almost over.

Salome reached into the crumpled mouth of the potato chip bag without touching it. Then, noiselessly, without causing a single tell-tale crack or crumpling sound, she withdrew a small, bubble-shaped potato chip. It fit the floor of her tongue perfectly.

Now it was hers. And it couldn't be his ever again.

She showed the potato chip on her tongue to the man who drove Dave's truck, as if she were presenting a small irreducible gift. Then she closed her mouth, chewed the potato chip, and swallowed.

"But maybe tomorrow we could talk about it," she conceded finally. Sometimes, you had to decide for them; it was too much responsibility for somebody who drove a truck. "But let's not tell Mrs Anderson. Because then Mrs Anderson will want to come too."

HOW SHE WAS SAVED

It was as if the world that once belonged to other people suddenly belonged to her too. She woke when she wanted, went to bed when she wanted, went to the kitchen and ate what she wanted, and went to the bathroom or walked to the park or drank juice when she wanted, and nobody tried to tell her otherwise – if she wanted to do something, she just did it. If she felt like Cheese Stix and pretzels for breakfast, she had Cheese Stix and pretzels for breakfast. If she felt like sleeping on a lawn chair in somebody's backyard, wrapped in the dog blanket and wearing a pair of stray, twisted earmuffs, then she slept in the yard wearing earmuffs. Sometimes, the people she lived with went away for days at a time and gave her full run of the house. She stayed up all night and slept all day with the television playing loud; she wrapped herself in shower curtains and danced in the tub. Her only responsibility was to show the owners of her temporary accommodation as much courtesy as they showed her. This meant never pestering them with personal questions about where they went or what they did when they got there.

"Hey, pumpkin!" they shouted as they came through the front door, laden with packages and suitcases, clattering with bottles and keys. Sometimes they called her "dollface," or "girl-kid," or "wild-child!" or "sport" (There was even one elderly white-haired gentleman, characteristically adorned in black linen suits and blond cashmere scarves, who enjoyed calling her "Lucy."). And they always brought gifts – special treats from the grocery store, dolls wrapped in crinkly plastic, or mammoth bathroom-scale-sized chocolate bars and super-hero comic books. "Did you miss us? Did you find everything you need? Look, we brought more of those Cheese Stix you like, and these really cheap kids-videos from a thrift store, featuring, let's see. This one's got Care Bears, and this one's got Snoopy. Have you ever seen a Snoopy cartoon, pumpkin? If you haven't seen Snoopy, you've never lived." Homecomings were Sal's favorite group activity with people she didn't know. It was as if, for these brief minutes and hours, everybody belonged together.

Lying together in front of the television, they stroked her hair while she curled in their laps like a huge, bony kitten, attired in forgotten bedclothes unearthed from dusty closets and attics. The clothes smelled like lilac soap, moth balls, and Ortho Snail repellent. It was probably Salome's favorite mixture of smells in the entire world.

"You have such lovely golden hair," they told her. The strokes of their raspy hands grew steadier and smoother with each passing beat. "Where did you get such silky soft hair like you've got? And your skin is so pink and new-looking, like you're this beautiful brand new silk comforter that's never been washed. How could we possibly have found such a delightful little creature walking alone on the highway and eating that dirty orange? Aren't you glad we found you, honey? Maybe someday we'll fix up your own room in the basement. Would you like your own room in the basement, honey? Just say the word and it's yours."

Often she fell asleep in their laps, but just as often they fell asleep first. The beat of their raspy fingers slowed and stopped. Their breathing subsided; they snored. The weight of their arms seemed to increase with their lassitude, as if only cork-like spirit buoyed them above the surface of dead matter, until Salome felt entangled and damp. She couldn't lift their arms; she could only twist, and shift, and create just enough imbalance in the overall engagement to pull herself free, withdrawing through that absence of force she always found in people if she looked hard enough. Then, when she finally stood apart from them, and the sound of her breathing was divorced from theirs, she could examine them objectively, like buildings through a coin-operated telescope, their mouths hanging open to expose gleaming gold teeth, dull-metal bridgework, and veiny, salivating tongues. It was like gazing into the future, Salome thought, looking into mouths like these. Deep pulsing caverns filled with creatures that were half-human, half-robot, and half something else entirely, humming and roving along predetermined pathways. Retrieving data, digging up rocks, initiating old functions. Performing the same tasks over and over again.

It wasn't like the movies where they left little girls bundled up on the doorsteps of benign, child-focused institutions with frosted windows and large bell-shaped brass door-knockers. Usually they just drove her to the edge of town and dropped her off with a tautly-packed brown grocery bag of supplies: a faded wool blanket, a bottle of water, several vacuum-sealed Lunchables, and a fully-intact bunch of seedless green grapes wrapped in wax paper. Then, more for their consolation than for hers, they ran through a checklist. For while people came in a variety of shapes, sizes, and religious orientations, they all liked filling out checklists. What they needed and brought with them; what they didn't need and could leave behind.

"Have you got a change of fresh clothes? And some of those breakfast bars you like?"

"Yes. Here. And more over here."

"Paper towels, antiseptic wipes, bandages? And the sheriff's number if anything bad happens, and a roll of quarters? Now tell me again. If anything bad happens, what do you do?"

"I call the Sheriff's Department."

"And if strangers try to touch you in an inappropriate fashion?"

"I ask them to stop. Then I call the Sheriff's Department."

"What about your diet? What do you need to remember?"

"Plenty of fresh fruit and vegetables. And one of my Flintstone vitamins every day. And whenever I go to the bathroom, wash my hands after."

"And don't get hysterical if something bad happens, or shut off and pretend it isn't happening. Tell me what you do if something bad happens."

"Don't get hysterical. Just pick up my stuff and walk away."

"That old sleeping bag has a minus-ten-degree comfort rating, so you should be fine through September. But if you're still in this part of the country when October comes around, you'll need more layers. It gets cold out here. Especially in the morning."

They sat in their cars letting the engine idle. Eventually, the sparks missed a beat. Sal didn't know much about cars, but she knew what she liked.

"I'll be fine," Sal told them. "Stop worrying. I've done this before."

At this point, they started to cry. It was very important to them: crying just long enough to show Salome they cared. Then they could stop crying and get on with their lives.

It isn't such a big deal, Sal wanted to tell them. This won't take as long as you think.

"I'll miss you, pumpkin," they would say, blowing their red noses into tattered wisps of Kleenex, and releasing the emergency brake with an autonomic little thunk. They didn't look back as they drove away, but sometimes they waved goodbye over their shoulder, perfunctory and candid, as if thanking another motorist for letting them into a busy lane.

"I'll miss you, too," Sal said softly, waving back to be polite. "Now please get out of here before I change my mind."

⸺

She slept in cornfields, off-road drainage tunnels, even a disused and crumbling army bunker or two. It was amazing, she thought, how many forgotten structures existed in the places where civilization doesn't matter. Broken fields of concrete, temblor-twisted railroad tracks, refuse-strewn deserts, and disused airport tarmacs – as if some terrific war had been secretly paved over by centuries of weather and neglect.

One night she slept in the broken-slatted bullpen of an overgrown baseball diamond. It was like stumbling onto an abandoned movie set, the torn lattices of high fences leaning overhead like the masts of some gigantic ghost-ship, cows and sheep grazing on the base paths like small clumps of landscape. Carrying her blanket down the weed-sprung concrete steps, she disturbed a family of what looked like ferrets. They darted, sudden and synchronous, a school of furry fish, in one smooth serpentine clatter over the splintery boards and vanished, poof. There was even a parchment-yellow, eczematic hardball sitting in a pool of greenish fluid. It said Berry Burlington in fine chicken-track red ballpoint ink, with big looping curlicues in the *B*'s and the *r*'s.

The bright full moon illuminated the ball park like civic-minded klieg lights, and Sal tried to imagine what people did in places like this. Maybe they laughed. Or ran shrieking from one torn, water-bloated base to another. Or swung wooden bats and hit balls with sudden, mighty cracks into the desert, or hurled them with sharp arm-whipping snaps into the humming moonlight. You had to find your way slowly through a world this wide and dark. It knew so much more than you did.

Before she went to bed that night, she washed her face with

two splashes of bottled Evian, and showed her lost baseball to the quietest, most contentedly-chewing of the piebald cows. They didn't sleep, these cows. Maybe it was a trick the full moon played on them. Or maybe it was just the nature of animals who lived on baseball diamonds.

"This baseball belonged to a little boy with big *B*'s in his name," she told the cow, without animosity or reproach. "But now the little boy and everybody who played with him are gone."

Some people, like Herb and Molly, lived in brand-new houses with brand-new matching carpets and drapes, where flakes of paper dust and pebbly packing material gave everything a faintly static look, as if you were watching television without cable. Outside, the fenceless yards joined together with other fenceless yards, and when you wandered into them, you found yourself looking into the picture windows of other people's houses, as if you were encircled by mirrors. It didn't matter what house you were in, since they all looked the same; they only approached the world from different directions. White clapboard walls, large wagon-wheel planters, gray concrete patios, red-brick barbecues, and thin pine saplings tied to wooden poles with green twine. They looked as new as Sal felt. They weren't impersonal; they were more like competition.

"If we call the cops," Herb said, "they turn her over to social services. And the things I've heard about social services, well. We might as well sell her to carnival people, or lock her in the attic with a bowl of water."

Once Molly had established Sal in a suitable chair at the too-large, brightly-varnished dining table, she set about doing the sorts of things these women frequently did. She wiped Sal's face with a damp, warm washcloth, combed her hair with a shining, gilt-edged comb from her vanity table, and delivered more food than Sal could eat, tidily arranged on white, floral-patterned china platters. Cheeses and crudités and bits of unidentifiable processed meat. Chopped-up apples and bananas and watermelons and pears. Slices of crustless white-bread spread with peanut butter, and tidy matching plastic containers of hummus, cole-slaw, potato salad, and tuna-whip.

"This is the first time I've tried this recipe," Molly told Sal, placing a bowl of soup in front of her, or a plate of pasta with sun-dried tomatoes and parsley. "This is the first time I've served anything on these new plates. My mother's cousin sent them after the wedding, probably because his wife died, and he doesn't want to be reminded about her anymore. It doesn't matter to me, though. Hundred-year-old full-serving china patterns don't grow on trees."

After dinner, they showed her around the slowly-forming new house, as pleased as real-estate brokers. The bedrooms with their big new beds and bare, recently-painted walls. The bathrooms inflated and hazy with gleaming porcelain and monogrammed white terrycloth towels. Or the nursery, inhabited by nothing more substantial than a promise – always the most finely-finished room in the house: the large wooden crib with bars like some primitive prison; the slowly turning mobiles of intriguing shapes and geometrical figures presiding over the empty mattress. The nursery decorations were always gender-neutral and inaccurate: happily smiling panda bears and goofily glowering, elongated giraffes. There was something about giraffes and panda bears that really excited these people. Probably because they were the types of people who only liked animals that never grew up.

But Sal's favorite place was always the basement. She kept opening doors until somebody said, "You don't want to go down *there*, sweetheart. It's just filled with old junk."

The best part about life was the part that happened when nobody was watching.

And the best place for living that life was always in the basements of other people's houses.

They always said the same things at breakfast.

"We can't keep her."

"I know we can't keep her. I was only saying."

"We don't even know when she was born. Maybe she should be in school already. Or what if she has a medical condition. A bad heart, or diabetes. What if she falls down and breaks her neck. We don't even know a decent pediatrician."

"I never said we should keep her. All I said was."

"You always want to take up lost causes, honey. It's what I love about you. But it leads to difficulties in the long term."

"All I meant was we should let her stay for a few days and see how it goes. Those are the exact words I used. I never said we should keep her."

While they talked, Sal spread jam on her toast. She preferred grape jelly, but few people seemed to use grape jelly anymore. They only seemed to have these squat, bulky jars of coagulated grapefruit that smelled like plastic-wrap.

"Just imagine if she turned out to be mentally ill. Like autistic or something. I spent enough of my life dealing with my sister, and you know how much dealing with Ellie screwed me up, honey. I don't know if I could go through those feelings again."

Sometimes the woman would just sit and watch Sal eat, thinking about the slowly circulating mobile upstairs in the untenanted nursery, holding the half-full coffee cup between her hands to keep warm. The women all had beautiful hands, Sal thought. Even when they weren't much to look at in the face-department.

"I don't think there's anything wrong with our little road bunny," the woman said. "Just watch her eat. She's so composed and attentive. Like she knows what's going on but can't be bothered. Like she's willing to leave the real job of living to everybody else."

The man would gather steam at this point, fueled by a secret purpose that had been growing all morning.

"Sometimes it takes years to tell if a child's autistic or not. You can't tell by looking at them, honey. Everything will be going along fine, then one day you find them cutting their wrists with the serrated steak knives, or bashing the cat with a rake. Usually, they do more damage to themselves than to anybody else, but that doesn't mean we shouldn't be careful. Ellie came completely unhinged a few times and I'll never forget those things she did in the bathroom. We don't want to go through that with your so-called 'road bunny.' Especially when she's not even related."

It was easier leaving in the middle of the night while they were still asleep; that way, she didn't have to deal with the treacly love-hugs and sobbing and spastic clutching that emerged from their bodies like errant strangers in an alley. It was as if they were trying to impress you with their dishonesty, or tangle you up in words. Oh my little darling my sweet little road baby please take care of yourself sweetheart we'll miss you *so much* and so forth. Even while you knew and they knew that they wanted you to leave quickly before they stopped wanting you to stay, it was so much more passionate for them this way, so much more beautiful to be in their house after you left than before you came. They had already thrown your blankets into the washing machine, and begun running the dishes from your "bon voyage" breakfast into the sudsing stainless steel dishwasher. They had already packed your lunch, and presented you some inconsequential gift to send you on your way, the one thing in the house Sal didn't want and couldn't wait to leave behind.

"Mr Midge was my bestest, favoritest friend when I was a little girl, and I want you to have him, and protect him, and all the while he'll be protecting you, and I'll know you'll always be safe."

They didn't just show you their tears – they spilled them all over you, wiping their snotty faces on your clean pink dress. Wrapping you up in their moisture as if they could take you into themselves, into that special place where they were looking forward to you going away.

" – and I just *know* you'll take good care of him, my little pillow-hugger, my little Cheese Stix lover. Because you're the sort of little girl who takes care of people, aren't you, my darling? You're not the selfish sort of girl who just wants other people to take care of *her* – "

It was the best time to see these neighborhoods: the streets devoid of strangers who might want her, nothing but a few forgotten toys on the lawns to remind Sal of the life she had observed through the windows of bedrooms and basements. The streetlights shone dimly all night long, illuminating things people weren't around to see. It was like self-consciousness alone with itself; the basic thrum of sentient, elemental matter. Aware of itself not being aware of itself being aware. In the vague moonlight, trees cast entanglements of leaves. Spots of faded oil sat on white driveways, waiting to swallow more darkness. I don't know much, Sal thought, walking down these half-lit streets in the middle of the night, sensing other spaces and dimensions out there – the abstract sketch of a mountain, the smell of brine from the sea – but I know what I know. And that's enough.

It wasn't life that persevered and spread across things – it was non-life, the great world-thing, deadness, stuff, raw hard reflective inorganic matter. Houses, mainly. Extending in every direction, thin and mutable and hollow and almost indistinguishable from one another and the things they kept inside. They spilled across plains like plastic tokens from a conveyor belt; they filled little glens and valleys and puddled in dewdrop-like housing communities and suburban-enterprise zones. They walled up rivers, climbed mountains, over-reached slopes and trees and rocks and anything that stood in their way. And if they couldn't eliminate it, they built themselves on top of it, gazing down serenely from stilts on brushy mountainsides, floating sedately on the lapping rims of cloudy bays and inlets, their hulls mossy and barnacled like very old men. Wherever Sal journeyed, these houses were always the first to see her coming and the last to see her leave. They were the only things that never said goodbye.

"Life never stood a chance," said the old man who ran the Beaver-Friendly Laundro-Dry in a desert-ringed town with a name like every other town – Desert Acres, or Littleton, or Bobville – Sal had no faith left in names. "It saw this stuff emerging from the world and just ran screaming. Houses, trucks, airplanes, fleets of buses and military vehicles, computers and satellite-dish TVs. This stuff about life being courageous and always finding a way? That's nonsense. Life is a sweet mistake that happened when the world wasn't looking. Now it's got to keep hiding and scurrying and burrowing and staying out of non-life's way. That's how the universe really works, honey. It takes things apart and puts them together again, which is perfectly okay if you're a piece of wood, but not so nice if you're a little girl trying to grow into a big one. Or even if you're an old man like me, and just trying to forget all the people you left behind."

Sal liked Laundromats; it was an affection she developed during her first winter, when she was growing cold and increasingly tired of other people's houses. In a Laundromat, she could sit for hours and watch the tumbling dryers, or flip through the tattered, sticky pages of magazines that grew on over-painted windowsills like plugs of lava from the fissures of a desert floor. Most of the magazines contained glossy pictures of young ladies who looked the way Sal felt. Detached, slightly petulant, gloaming with fabric and conditioners, they stood in awkward poses, their heads cocked at odd angles to perceive a world beyond the one that kept perceiving them. They wore nighties and mink coats and black lash-strapped high-heels and smoked cigarettes in long slender ivory holders. They stroked the hoods of purring black automobiles, and dived into blue pools in golden swimsuits, and flew kites on the beach, fully attired in fashionable percale knitwear. Sometimes the girls were accompanied by very feminine-looking men with sharp cheekbones who wore nice leather jackets and bell-bottom trousers. These men were often prettier than the women. They wore simpler, more tastefully-appointed jewelry.

"That pile of magazines is like an archeological dig reaching back into pre-history and beyond. You've got written materials in there going all the way back to a time when even *I* was good looking." The old man was always sweeping, mopping, and wiping surfaces with a faded brick-red cotton rag, or pushing squeaky laundry carts from one end of the fluorescent room to another, while somebody's soft-soled shoes thumped inconstantly in the dryer like noisy neighbors. "I'm afraid to touch it; I might invoke nameless forces. Dead celebrities and politicians – you don't get more cosmic than that. Endless recipes for casseroles, fondue, and veal. That's where non-life comes from, little girl; from the deepest substrata of old magazines and newspapers. If you dig deep enough, you can get so lost you forget yourself altogether. And personally, little girl, I don't think that would be a bad idea. If I didn't have so much mopping, I'd probably go down there with you. I'd get as far away from myself as I could."

———

The old man slept on a fold-out cot in a secret storage room behind the bank of dryers, with bare-beamed walls thumbtacked over by yellowing wall calendars and tattered tourist flyers of Mauritius. "It's the best job in the world," he liked to say. "I get to be around people, and hardly ever talk to them. And whenever they ask questions, I've got all the answers, just like one of those Mr Know-it-all-subscription-time guys on a PBS pledge drive. Questions like where's the change machine? Or I can't use that change machine that change machine's busted. And I just point to the sign that says Customers are Required to Provide Their Own Coinage, or if I really don't like them, I point to the other, comical one that says We Reserve the Right to Send Your Ass Packing. Or they might ask how much bleach they should use, and I say I don't know, I'm not the Bleach Man, or how much detergent, and I say I don't know, I'm not the Detergent Man. Or my favorite question, which is probably: isn't there a Friendly's around here? Which is when I lean the mop against my shoulder and tell them, Sure is, Charlie. You'll never *find* a Laundromat in this state without a Friendly's nearby. Because when you get right down to it, that food's *designed* for people waiting for the dry cycle to end. You'd have to be crazy to go there otherwise."

A Laundromat possessed no definable substance or sense of itself, and since it didn't exist anywhere specific, Sal never felt the urgency to dispatch herself anywhere else. At night, she and the old man shared meals of cheese-cracker sandwiches, salted peanuts, and cheddar-flavored popcorn from the vending machine, which the old man opened with a key from his belt. Then they finished off an assortment of candy bars, plastic-wrapped mini-pies, and suckable hard-candies. "The trick is to drink a load of this mineral water, both at the start and at the end of every meal," the old man told her. He was leading her in a toast with a corrugated blue-tinted plastic bottle. "That's good, chug it down. Water cleanses the body of all the crap that builds up during the day. Which means you can spend the rest of the day loading your body up with lots more of the selfsame crap. That's my personal philosophy of body maintenance, anyway. Don't be afraid of pleasing yourself. But make sure you pay the price before going to bed."

The old man never told Sal what to do or think, so it wasn't like living with someone, or hiding behind somebody else's notion of who you were. At his most pedantic, he sat beside her in one of the cracked orange plastic chairs and showed her the keys on his belt, one at a time, which Sal considered an experience almost mystical in its intensity. "Coin trays for the dryers," he would say, showing her one key. "Coin trays for the washer," showing her another. "Vending machine, you've seen that. Front door. Back door. Storage room. Don't know what this does. Don't know what this does either. This does the cashbox, and this does the mailbox at UPS. Don't know what this does – think I used to, but not sure anymore. And this one, I think it belonged to a car I once owned. Can't remember what sort of car either, but a big one. A real gas-guzzler."

***

Best of all, the old man never asked Sal questions, which was the main quality about him that convinced her to stay. Everything he said was devoid of condition, truthfulness, or opinion.

"You could sleep here on these chairs, if you want. We could make up a little cot from these old sheets and towels. You wouldn't believe the stuff people leave behind, entire washers and dryers full of bedclothes, dresses, denim trousers, you name it. Look, here's a pink dress almost like the one you're wearing. Only it's really clean and fresh-smelling, see. I keep all this stuff in a well-maintained state, little girl. Because you never know when something will come in handy, or what you'll need for the next rainy day."

The padded benches along one wall could be unlocked with one of the old man's keys, divulging carefully organized categories of things in angular wooden boxes. Paperback books with torn, sticky covers; a shoebox full of marbles; a wicker hamper filled with stuffed dolls and animals; and a clear glass jar, thick and dusty with foreign coins, metal washers, and plastic jewelry, like the terrarium of some wind-up mechanical lizard.

"Anything you find in there is yours," the old man said, as he assembled a thick mattress on the bank of scoop-backed orange plastic chairs. "I can't let you sleep with me because I snore, and that wouldn't be fair to either of us. To you, for your inalienable right to a good night's sleep. Or to me, for my equally inalienable right to make as much goddamn noise as I feel like. Just look at all these dollies and toys and stuff and old record albums. Take your pick. But try to put everything back where you found it. If you don't keep stuff organized, it takes over your life. And once stuff takes over your life, you might as well cash in your chips. They'll be sweeping you out from behind the dryers, honey. They'll be dumping you in the trash with all these old magazines."

It wasn't hard, Sal thought, knowing what you wanted. And it was so much easier to know what you wanted when you were sitting in a Laundromat with an old man like this one.

So she showed him.

"Is that really all, little girl? How about one of those board games. Or the jigsaw puzzles. I put an Elmo jigsaw puzzle in there once. I just can't remember where."

For an old man who talked too little, Sal thought, sometimes he talked too much. So she showed him again.

He had just finished patting her mattress in place. White sheets and cotton blankets – thick, pleated, seamed. He turned to Sal and shrugged his thin knobby shoulders.

"Of course you can have it, little girl. And from now on, any pink dress I find that comes *close* to your size? Well, that baby's *already* yours."

At night, the old man's snores reverberated through the sheet-metal frames of appliances like vast subterranean forces, earthquakes or volcanoes. They made the windows rattle in their frames, and the lids of the padded benches chatter. Lying at night in the glass-walled Laundromat, supine on her makeshift mattress, Sal felt part of the world but not of it. The dead trees outside, the moon, the sniffing rib-framed dogs, and urgently-mating cats – they all occurred distantly like the gears and levers of a gigantic mechanical clock, the sort you wind up until you can't wind it any further.

In the morning, Sal would fold up the individual sheaves and pallets of her mattress and replace them in their appropriate storage chests. Then she would change into her clean pink dress, and take the soiled pink dress she had removed to the cylindrical chamber of the Jumbo washer, crank shut the door, and activate it with a spare set of keys the old man had recovered from a high rusty hook in the store room. She would set it to Delicate Wash – Fine Fabric, apply minimal doses of detergent and fabric softener, and sit in front of the large, cyclops-like machine, patiently observing it through its cycles, the way cautious parents observe their children on a merry-go-round at the park. Hissing, sudsing, roaring, and then spinning with a benign thunderous clatter, even more ferocious and unstoppable than the old man snoring. She took it to the dryer, fluffed and folded, and by the time the old man woke and came into the Laundromat in his baggy sweatpants and fishnet T-shirt, she was already sitting on the same bank of chairs where she had slept, swinging her legs back and forth, wearing one clean pink dress and holding the tidy folded packet of the other in her lap, fingering the white lacy collar, or examining the chiffon cuffs and hems for loose threads, which she bit off with sharp, perfunctory snaps of her front teeth. Tomorrow, she thought, I'll wear this dress and wash the one I'm wearing. It was the most delicious and unaccountable sensation she had ever known.

"Pink's definitely a nice color on you," the old man told her one morning while he swept ropes of blue lint from behind the dryers. "Not because it's girly or anything, but because there's something clean and rosy about it, just like you. But at the same time, and I hope this doesn't sound critical, I'll bet there are lots of nice colors that would look pretty on you. For instance, I've got some denim pants your size in that drawer over there. Or this robe-like white cotton thing, decorated with pandas and giraffes. And in that other bench, I'm pretty sure we've got some of those T-shirts with super heroes on them, they're perfectly female-type super heroes, don't get me wrong. Like Super Lady, or the Sexy Girls, super heroes like that. And maybe some shoes, you should look through the shoe assortment and find yourself another pair, like tennis shoes or something. Those pink dressing-up ones look like they been through the wars and lost everyone they loved. They're not functional. And there's something about you, little girl, that definitely needs functional shoes."

Sometimes, realization came out of nowhere, just when you thought there was nothing left to learn. Sal watched the old man transferring lumps of lint into a large white plastic trash receptacle. On the surface, he resembled the same old man as always. He was disregarding her the same way he always did.

My shoes, she thought. Shoes that aren't me. Shoes that are me.

Suddenly the old man was no longer somebody who didn't notice Sal. But Sal was somebody who had learned to notice him.

———

Laundromats were perfect, though, and Sal made certain the next one was fully automated, allowing her to settle down permanently for the first time since losing Daddy. Little girls in pink dresses weren't noticed in places like these, where people were always coming and going with children and dogs that might or might not belong to them. All Sal had to do to make a space hers was sit on a vinyl-padded bench, or in a cracked orange plastic chair, and fold her arms with a sense of inward concentration. Nobody else's. Just hers. Whether other people liked it or not.

For the first time in her life, Sal didn't have to go looking for people, or leave them behind when they grew frivolous. Instead, people were always coming towards her and walking past as if she didn't register, hefting lumpy pillow-cases packed with soiled linens like shabby Santas, or bearing big wicker baskets overflowing with cottony fabrics, and sloshing around primary-colored tubs of detergent and bleach. They nattered into their cell phones about personal issues or where they put the mayonnaise or when they'd catch the next bus, or peered into the *USA Today* crossword, or ate packaged meals from fast food restaurants laid out in their laps like road atlases. Meanwhile their anonymous children – wild, half-formed, useless, and deeply inappropriate for every worldly condition – constantly banged things for attention, or stained their faces with purple juice-like substances. They hid under chairs and benches and watched each other like wolves watching mice. But none of them possessed the intensity of wolves, or would know what to do with a mouse if they caught one.

Sometimes they circled Sal from a distance, or paraded back and forth while examining her with long, attenuate faces, their eyes blank as windshields. Eventually, the wildest and smallest would sit on a nearby chair and show her something like a votive offering. A cap pistol, a topless plastic doll, a palm-sticky bottle cap, a bug in a jar. Something obvious; they weren't really trying.

"No, thank you," Sal told them, without looking up. She didn't want to encourage them. They probably received too much encouragement as it was. "I wouldn't know what to do with it if you paid me."

Then she lifted the folded pink dress from her lap and showed it to them.

"I've got everything I need right here."

There were lots of places to sleep in a Laundromat, but Sal preferred the big bench-seats, their dark, splintery interiors littered with crumpled gray burlap sacks, twisted unidentifiable bits of metal and crusty mouse droppings. It was like hiding inside your own body, or abandoning the world to escape with all your plenitude. Sometimes, her head propped against an old tire or a rust-stained paper bag filled with six-inch nails, Sal fell asleep and dreamed of Daddy in his white van, bumping over hard things in the road, his voice continuous, unremitting, and strong: "I'll love you just as much. I'll try just as hard. Anything you want. It's already yours." It was more than those wolfish children could ever hope for, preoccupied with their grubby bits of wood, lozenge-sized pencil sharpeners, and tattered, hand-worn bags of jelly-candies. Launched into a world without sadness, carried away by somebody so strong they could make you theirs simply by finding you. Somebody who loved you more than anybody ever loved you before.

But until Daddy found her again, Sal would have to be content with her secret space inside the wooden bench, lying awake each night, breathing the musty odors of herself and awaiting the nightly arrival of the Unhappy Man.

His car made a large pop when it arrived at the front door, like a gunshot on TV. The Unhappy Man was just a series of breathing sounds at first, banging into things and pushing them aside. His feet shuffled across the scuffed linoleum with a fierce, slovenly beat, as if he were disputing every step across the world he didn't want to know. "The stupid hairy little bitch," he said, swinging open doors until they screeched on rusty hinges. "Lying around all day, staring at that goddamn TV." His keys sounded louder and more unanimous than those of the old man, and he shook them at every lock that came his way – dryers, vending machines, storage rooms, secret doors, and metal lockboxes.

"She'll eat what I give her, I'm not a fucking five-star chef. She'll eat it and like it," he told the Laundromat, which gathered identity and temper whenever he appeared, like a spider emerging from a hole in the ground. "Giving me those looks, eating me out of house and home. Goddamn bitch with her love magazines and her cookies. One goddamn cookie she could leave me, but no, she couldn't leave me just one goddamn cookie. That would be too much to ask."

As the Unhappy Man approached the bench in which she lay hidden, Sal felt herself growing more compact and real. Nobody could find her. Nobody knew she was here. There was just her, the darkness, and the roving coherence and clumsy immensity of the Unhappy Man.

"I'll lock her in the basement next time." Silver coins spilled into dull metal pails. Flimsy metal doors scraped open and shut. Then the footsteps again, angry at themselves, overturning every stone but Sal's. "She'll learn her lesson then, boy. She'll stop leaving hairs all over the carpet. Or I'll lock her in the basement and throw away the key."

Every morning, Sal was woken by the systematic beeping of garbage trucks, reversing themselves into blind alleys, heaving up hidden car-sized bins with robot-like appendages. It was the providence Sal had learned to expect from everyday objects, that infinite web of destiny, mercy, and grace that protected her from the stress and inconstancy of people who wanted to save you until they found something better to do.

"She must be the manager's daughter," people whispered when they saw her unlocking machines or coin boxes with the loose collection of keys she had gathered from the sepulchral, almost polyhedral storage room, which was left unlocked every few nights or so by the Unhappy Man. "She certainly knows her way around, and where to find quarters. She's so careful about her appearance; she must brush her teeth after every meal. Maybe that's why this place is such a wreck. The owners spend all their time looking after this beautiful little girl. They don't have time for customers. They probably believe, quite rightly, that family comes first."

Some keys were bent and misshapen. Others, when you washed them under the store-room tap, shone like gold.

"Little girl? Can I ask you a question?"

Sal never said anything unless she had to. It was the best method she knew for preserving integrity and self-control.

"When's your daddy coming back?"

Sometimes you had to give them a glimpse. If only to preserve the integrity of everything you didn't want to tell them.

"Sometime soon."

"I need to speak to him. Can you put me in contact with him right away?"

"I usually wait around and he comes. I don't contact him. He always contacts me."

"He can't be gone long, can he? I mean, he wouldn't just leave his little girl sitting around a Laundromat, would he?"

Sal shrugged. It was the only thing you could tell some people. Then she unpeeled the aluminum-lined wrapper of her Power Bar. Power Bars were like candy bars, only good for you. Somebody had told her this a long time ago.

"I lost my five dollar bill in that machine. Maybe your daddy could open it with one of his keys and get me my five dollars back."

These women were the opposite of the women who lived in new houses. They were large, bulkily formed, and poorly dressed, resembling the pillowcases full of laundry they hauled in from their smoking, over-size cars with twisted fenders and crepitating vinyl hoods. They lit endless streams of cigarettes, one off the other, and when they finished, flicked them out the door into the rainy gutter with audible sighs, as if they had just received a terrible news flash about old friends. They ate crinkle-cut potato chips and drank from liter bottles of diet soda. Sal wouldn't be caught dead spending the night with women like these. They would take everything she had and never give anything back.

Sal examined the label on her Power Bar. Numbers were good when you could get them, but words were always better.

"If I could call my daddy anytime I wanted," Sal said, without looking up, "then I wouldn't be here, would I? I'd be with him, and we'd already be on our way to somewhere else."

According to Sal's estimate, the Unhappy Man had been coming to the Laundromat for more than a hundred years, locking the place up every night and unlocking it every morning, and during that time he had systematically managed to forget, misplace, or leave behind everything valuable that he possessed. A gold watch with a torn leather wrist band; random utility bills imprinted with circular coffee stains and crystallized boogers; three identical photographs of a very old woman standing in front of a redwood with her arms posed in a mocking flourish, as if she were indicating some ridiculous stage prize on "The Price is Right"; a glass jar filled with quadrangular runic coins; and countless tiny wads of white paper, which lay sprinkled across the floors of the storage room like lumpy artificial snow on a cheap sound stage. How could anybody afford to lose so much of themselves? Sal wondered, hugging her spare pink dress to her chest, standing alone at night in the empty Laundromat and leaning from side to side to the slow sway of music emanating from an unseen juke box several streets away. Wouldn't it make you feel hollow? Wouldn't you expire and collapse, your features misshapen, like a deflating Jack-O-Lantern three days after Halloween? At night, the dryers gazed benevolently down from their frozen chromatic banks like computer consoles on an interstellar space ship, deprived of contact with any organic life form besides Sal.

"There's nothing left in this goddamn country worth wasting our youth on," said Tim, a young man who worked morning shifts at Store 24. "Which is because the previous generation took everything that wasn't nailed down and disappeared into South Carolina retirement-heaven, where they're now playing golf and shuffleboard year-round while *we* sell Sausage-Dogs and Big Gulps to road maintenance workers and drug-addicts. Just look around, little girl, and what do you see? Bankrupt strip malls, tattoo-parlors, and topless clubs on one side of the fence – and on the other? A lot of over-priced condos and chlorinated swimming pools. And how many young people my age do you see living on the *quality* side of the fence? Not many, that's for sure. Most of us are working minimum wage in stupid jobs like this one, and living with our grandmas. Take me, for example. My parents didn't want to look at me anymore, and remind them of my wasted opportunities, so they split. Said they didn't like my "hostile attitude." Said they didn't like my "negative self-image factor." Now they live in, you guessed it, South Carolina, with all the other people who ran this stupid country into the ground. And they can take their positive self-image values and shove them up their you-know-whats, so far as I'm concerned. Me and Grandma are going to be fine without them. I don't know how, but one way or another, we'll manage."

Sal budgeted herself to eight quarters per day, which was usually more than she needed. An apple or a banana; a box of animal cookies; a carton of juice. "All the essentials," Tim told her, totting up her minimal purchases on the loudly ruminating cash register. "Vitamins, minerals, roughage – and just enough tiger-shaped cookies for biting off heads. The body can't live by bread alone, little girl. It needs to grab a pair of those tigerish cookie-haunches in its teeth and take a perfect, well-formed bite. It needs to do damage to something that isn't itself. That's a buck-seven, but here, take these pennies from the penny-jar, and it comes to one buck even. That's perfectly good legal American currency, little girl, and look what most people do with it. They dump it in some stranger's jar and never look back."

Standing at the counter of Store 24 every morning was like haunting the intersection of another dimension, where vaguely misdirected men in striped uniform jerseys, torn jeans, and wide-brimmed baseball caps somnabulistically activated the chiming door-scanners, stood watch over the crooked and loosely-jointed magazine racks, and purchased cigarettes, reformed salty beef byproducts, and neon-like lottery tickets which they called out over the counter like lazy Hallelujahs at a dispiriting and endless church service. Big Picks, Lucky Draws, Quick Dips, Scratch and Wins, Magic Sevens, the Big Haul, a litany of hugeness which dwindled into itself with each pronouncement, like a stellar breeze sucked into its own vanishing.

"It's like we've given up on everything, especially any notion of collective life," Tim said. Sometimes, when the shop was empty, he followed her outside and sat on the curb, paying just enough attention that she couldn't leave. "There's no place to sit down and talk, and nobody to talk to if there was. Everybody's working shit-ass jobs, or wandering vaguely through monolithic shopping complexes filled with processed meats and cheeses, and nobody has anything in common with anybody else, because who wants to share the secret knowledge that we're all the same? We're all going nowhere. We all live with our grandmas. And it won't get any better until we're dead. Like I saw this career guidance-counselor at my college yesterday, a nice lady named Mrs Ramirez, and according to her I can look forward to either teaching unruly school kids the things I didn't want to learn when I was their age, or guide desperate people through loan applications over the phone. It's like the future keeps getting smaller every day. And it's taking us with it."

Some mornings, she found him asleep in his car, a dented Plymouth Sundance with racing stripes and a broken-backed passenger seat, the interior windshield still vaporous from last night's cigarettes. Sometimes she took his striped jersey and brown corduroy pants inside to wash them while he sat running the engine and listening to Don Imus on the dashboard radio, wrapped up in one of the stray paisley fitted sheets from Sal's makeshift mattress, and eating cookies from the all-bountiful Vend-O-Mat. "Love is not a physical experience, little girl," he explained. "It's more a matter of two souls adapting to one another over time and space. I don't expect you to kiss me, or hug me, or even stroke my hair. I just want you to spiritually develop along lines that are appropriate to my personal lifestyle agenda."

And so he began to bring her things she didn't need, and when she showed him she didn't need them, he took them away again in his car, or dumped them in the back seat with the crumpled newspapers and baseball magazines, the large spine-broken textbooks of anatomy, sociology, and global telecom-munications he kept as mementos of his expiring education. He brought her fading photos of childhood pets and sweethearts, plastic bowling trophies for Best High Score and Highest Aver-age, paperback books featuring wolves with glowing red eyes on their creased, water-stained covers, and green plastic hard-bitten toy soldiers that he kept in a gallon-sized cookie jar, embossed with glue-stains and the hazy remains of a peeled-away white label.

"For the first few years, we'll get to know each other intellectually," he explained, as if he were mapping an expedition into the African interior. "Then we'll conform to one another physically, like gloves to hands, or shoes to feet. Like let's say you decide to be an artist and live in the desert, and do this whole Georgia O'Keefe deal; then I'll have to accept that I can't be an arctic explorer, or a foreign correspondent. I adjust to you, and you adjust to me. Throughout the course of our life, we'll come into lots of conflicts like that, but we'll always work things out and make our love stronger. That's because you and I possess synergy, little girl. Which means we're more together than the sum of our parts. We're meant to be together, whether anybody else likes it or not."

Tim never entered the Laundromat or asked questions about her former life, so if Sal was expected to love somebody when she grew up, it might as well be him. Tim was a boy and she was a girl. Tim was big and she was small. Tim had a place in the world where he conversed with other people, and Sal had a place in the world where she didn't. And since they possessed so many dissimilar qualities at the same time, they might as well possess them together. Every morning, Sal went to Store 24 during his shift and spent no more than her self-allotted eight quarters. But she never told him about the Unhappy Man, and she never told him about Daddy. It was the perfect arrangement for two people planning to grow old together.

On Halloween morning, it snowed, forming hard little islands of knobby ice around abandoned cars in the parking lot, and when she arrived at Store 24 wearing a striped flannel pillowcase over her pink dress – holes torn for her head and arms like the alb of some revolutionary priest – Tim invited her to dinner. "I'll pick you up at six," he said, "as soon as I get out of class. And don't bother bringing anything, unless there's something you want besides wine or tap water. Grandma doesn't keep sugary drinks around the house on account of her medicine."

Being driven in Tim's car wasn't like transportation; it felt more like staring out the window at another world going away. The entire car trembled – latches, seat frames, undercarriage, and something round, steel-like, and unstable in the gas tank, like a large iron caster in a dented iron bucket. The windshield wipers flapped brokenly against a gray, translucent mist that grew thicker with each beat, and the dashboard fans generated more noise than heat. In the woods, even the high beams lost focus and determination, as if you needed to forget where you were going in order to get there.

"Now there're a couple things I need to warn you about Grandma," Tim said, wiping the inside of the windshield with a faded gray dishrag. "Firstly, she's like totally coherent in most of her mental faculties, but you can't always tell because of her teeth. Another thing is she's very protective of me, her only surviving grandson, since I'm all she's got left, so let's not even mention the possibility we'd elope. If she's not friendly at first, she warms up after a while. And once she gets to know you like I do, she'll be more supportive of our relationship. A lot of people in this world just have dirty minds when it comes to meaningful human relationships, but not Grandma. Grandma's been around the block a few times. She doesn't judge others, and she doesn't like being judged."

There were no streetlights out here, just a few reflective aluminum pie tins nailed to trees and fence-posts. When they drove down a long, sparsely-graveled driveway to the two-story, single-gabled house, a dog started barking far away, as if trying to get their attention. Tim turned off the ignition; the motor kicked loosely for several seconds. Then, for the first time since they met, Tim took Sal's hand.

"It's nothing fancy," he whispered. "Just fish sticks, corn dogs, and frozen peas. The most important thing is: don't let her frighten you. She's a pretty odd old bat, even on her good days."

———

Grandma was sitting on a scratchy osier sofa in a blue bath-robe, staring at a hardback-sized transistor radio on a table. A loop of twisted coat hanger had been jammed into the nub of the broken antenna. Grandma's toothless mouth hung open, with a strange disregard for propriety, and her left hand, clenched and veiny in her lap, was the heaviest, solidest, and most substantial thing about her. Grandma continually massaged the clenched fist with her leaner, more adept hand, as if comforting a pet. She was the thinnest person Sal had ever seen, and her skull resembled a stippled raw pink bathing cap underneath her sparse, recently-permed hair.

"I tried to help with her makeup," Tim said sadly. "But I didn't do a very good job."

Grandma didn't speak until Tim snapped off the thirties-style band music on her transistor radio. And then she said:

"Ahhhhhh. *Ahhhhhhhhh*."

While Tim unfolded three aluminum TV trays and set them in a circle next to the radio, Grandma worked a purple tongue in her wide, round mouth as if she were churning butter.

"Ahhhhhhhhh," Grandma said.

"Grandma's telling you about her stroke," Tim said. He placed a perforated paper towel on Sal's lap without touching her; he seemed shy about their awkward moment in the car. "And how she hasn't been herself since we lost her teeth at the bowling alley."

"Ahhhhhhhhh," Grandma said.

Tim brought white plates from the kitchen, one at a time. Ketchup, mayonnaise, and a 16-ounce tub of soft-margarine.

"She wants to know if you've been married." Tim turned his back to Grandma and winked at Sal. "Just play along. I can never tell if she's kidding or not."

"No," Sal said. She picked up a charred fish stick and examined it. "I'm only four years old." She thought about the fish stick for a moment and replaced it beside the blotch of ketchup on her plate. "Or maybe five. I'm not entirely sure."

"Ahhhhhh."

Tim finished serving. He sat down and began cutting Grandma's fish sticks into small quadrangular chunks with a fork. "Now she's saying nice things about me, singing my praises," he said, without looking up. "If she wasn't my Grandma, I'd be flattered. Saying what a great guy I am, blah blah, how I'm so hardworking and all. But of course that's what Grandmas are *supposed* to say when they meet their future grand-daughter-in-law. She's just doing what grandmas are *supposed* to do."

After Tim dropped her off at the Laundromat, Sal stood alone in the parking lot, feeling landlocked and obvious. The dead cars had been towed away, leaving behind exhaust-smudged punctuations of knobby gray ice, and even before she approached the Laundromat's fingerprint-streaked glass doors she sensed the articulation of bolts within doorframes, hard and intemperate. It was like standing outside an aquarium, gazing at all that blueish, malformed light and refracted stillness, and for a while Sal enjoyed the sense of distinction it loaned her, simple objective comprehension of the spaces she had left behind. Tim's house, on the other hand, possessed many rooms filled with cardboard boxes and broken, water-stained lamps. If she got to know Tim better, he might show her the basement. The basement would be marvelous in a house like that.

Standing in the parking lot, Sal felt the future take shape in her mind. Tim and Grandma and the basement. Driving by the Laundromat in Tim's car. Her keys hidden in the bench where she had left them earlier tonight, an always-ripe memory of plenitude. The Unhappy Man driving around and around in his car, lost in somebody else's orbit, never sure where he was going or if he had arrived there or not. Routine bodies orbiting other bodies. Everybody journeying endlessly through the same universe whether they liked it or not.

Slowly, snowflakes began to fall, one after another, then in threes and fours, then in hundreds and thousands, whirling with bright escalating intensity. They bit at Sal's arms and face like tiny insects, without greed or supposition. They delivered nothing more or less than the simple meaning of themselves.

"We can only have one home at a time," Sal said out loud, as the flurrying snow wrapped her up in its world of the invisible. "But if we're not ready to appreciate it, or we forget the keys, then we can't have any home at all. We have to get moving. We have to start all over again."

THE BOOK OF PEOPLE

"Some people suffer painful, traumatic events they remember all their lives," Mrs Mayhew explained several weeks later in her cluttered, windowless office at the State Child Benefits Agency, a white block-like pre-fab building on the main street of a thin town punctuated by very blue lakes and very green trees. "But at other times, they suffer events which are so painful they can't remember them on account of something we call Traumatic Shock Syndrome. Traumatic Shock Syndrome is a very mysterious ailment we are only just beginning to understand, a super-serious form of repression that afflicts even little girls like yourself. To put it simply, sometimes bad things happen to us so often, and so predictably, that we learn to ignore them, or lock them behind a big black door so they can't frighten us. Maybe these experiences are physically painful, or emotionally painful. They might involve actual beasts and monsters – people who do unexplainable things to us for no apparent reason. But just as often, these experiences involve *imaginary* beasts and monsters, like bad dreams, or horrible stories we're told about who we are. When we learn to live with this abuse so proficiently that we direct it against ourselves, it initiates something I like to call Self Abuse Steady-State Syndrome, a variation on Traumatic Shock Syndrome that hasn't been accepted by the closed-minded professional community at large. But let's face it. Not being accepted by the professional community at large is a pretty common cross to bear when you're a social scientist. It's something you learn to live with if you want to keep thinking outside the box."

They were sitting on opposite sides of Mrs Mayhew's varnished desk, upon which several manila folders were arrayed like an enormous tableau of playing cards, their brightly-inscribed plastic tabs referring unashamedly to various capitalized Cases that had been assigned (like Sal) to Mrs Mayhew's unwavering attention and control. Case-4223, Case-St-317, Case-Anon2004. The slenderest of these files lay open, revealing a single sheet of paper that Mrs Mayhew wasn't looking at. Height, weight, age, eye color, hair – Sal couldn't bear to look. It made her feel obvious. Having her vital statistics included among these folders was the closest thing to a sense of community Sal had ever known.

She only hoped she wouldn't have to know it much longer.

Mrs Mayhew looked slightly frazzled, like an undone shoelace. Her glasses were cocked at a strange angle, as if she were peering sideways at herself.

"I'm not saying that taking a journey deep into your own psyche is going to be easy, Stephanie. But it will definitely be more productive than bottling things up inside. Denial closes you off from healthy, permanent relationships with other people. I'm saying that I want to help you, Stephanie, and stand beside you, no matter how long it takes. Will you accept my offer of assistance? I promise to support any decision you choose to make – whether I agree with that decision or not."

Set apart from the general clutter of Mrs Mayhew's desk stood a framed photo of a golden-haired retriever gripping a blue rubber ball in its teeth. It was clearly a nice dog, Sal thought. And definitely more interesting to look at than Mrs Mayhew.

Mrs Mayhew smiled for the first time since they met. It was like the wind shifting on a frozen lake.

"Her name is Madame Butterfly. Do you think that's a funny

name for a dog, Stephanie? I mean, naming it after a butterfly and all?"

Sal took her eyes away from the photograph. At this point, she didn't have any choice but to look at Mrs Mayhew.

"I guess," Sal said slowly. Her pink hands were framed by the cradle of her plain white cotton smock, issued to her on the day she was brought here from County Hospital. You had to think quickly with a woman like Mrs Mayhew.

"But then most dogs have funny names," Sal said after a while. "It's just the way dogs are."

***

Sal endured several private sessions in Mrs Mayhew's office, where they shared cold glasses of water and thin bologna sandwiches. Most of these sessions involved long, rambling disquisitions from Mrs Mayhew concerning appropriate eating and grooming habits for little girls, recently-viewed movies and television programs featuring "normal" relations between children and adults, and hastily snapped, poorly-lit photographs of people from Sal's immediate past. Examining these photos – which Mrs Mayhew didn't present for consideration so much as spring upon Sal like the punch lines of jokes – was like looking through the windows of a doll house at somebody else's dolls.

"Here's an interesting person who lives in our town," Mrs Mayhew explained one day, producing a cardboard-backed photo from a stack in her lap and snapping it down on the table, as if declaring "Gin!" at a garden party. "Her name is Ellen Mitchell Davidson, and she used to work at a primary school in New Hope. Once a widely respected civic leader, with strong links to the Methodist community, she cut herself off from all human contact when her husband died in '79. According to her neighbors, she grew withdrawn, sullen, and incapable of driving to the local market without hitting either a hydrant or a hedge.

Now take a look at this picture for me, Stephanie, and tell me what you know about Ellen Mitchell Davidson. Did you ever spend any time with her? Did she ever ask you to do anything you didn't want to do?"

The picture was like a cartoon of Grandma, her blotchy pink skin streaking the harsh background like a thin coat of beige paint. Her hard, small eyes looked surprised and deeply illuminated, as if somebody had inserted a flashlight through cloth flaps in the back of her head. It was hard for Sal to imagine this ageless husk of a woman removed from the well-adapted contours of her house. It didn't seem fair. Grandma deprived of her grandma-ness.

But Sal knew the drill. If she talked about other people, then she didn't have to talk about herself. It wasn't betrayal; it was self-defense.

"I just knew her as Grandma," Sal offered after a while, wishing there was a clock in Mrs Mayhew's office. She had never thought about wishing for clocks before, but now she couldn't stop. "She lives in the woods. She doesn't have pets, and she doesn't cook. I never knew her name was Ellen Mitchell Davidson. But if you tell me that's her name, then I guess I believe you."

Mrs Mayhew looked straight into Sal's eyes; then, with a little ocular tug, drew a line from Sal's eyes to the person in the photograph, as if threading a needle.

"For many years," Mrs Mayhew explained, "this woman you call 'Grandma' worked with children from many walks of life. Many of these children were little girls such as yourself, with happy-go-lucky outlooks and healthy behavioral strategies. Unbeknownst to their parents and legal guardians, these happy little girls went to school expecting to be taught important things by this so-called 'Grandma.' They placed their faith in her, and respected her pronouncements. And whenever she told these children to do something, they did it. However surprising or distasteful, her pronouncements were accepted at face value because they were issued by a person of 'importance.' Now, just for the fun of it, Stephanie, let's play a little game. Let's pretend you're one of these little girls I'm talking about, and I'm not Mrs Mayhew anymore. Instead, I'm the woman you call 'Grandma.' Can you do that for me, Stephanie? You'll notice I'm awaiting your direct confirmation before we proceed. That's because I don't want to do anything you don't want me to do."

Sal sucked on her tongue for a moment. Since coming to live in this large house with Mrs Mayhew, she had developed a secret taste for herself.

"I guess that would be all right," Sal said.

Sometimes Mrs Mayhew peered at Sal across the table as if she were trying to see through a slim, barely perceptible slit in Sal's forehead.

"Thank you very much," Mrs Mayhew said. "Now, if you don't mind, let's proceed."

The games were slow to get started, but then moved along briskly.

"Good afternoon, Stephanie. Would you like to sit in my lap? Would you like me to stroke your hair?"

"No, thank you, Grandma."

"Would you like me to give you a bath? Or tuck you into bed?"

"I don't believe I would like a bath right now." Sal thought for a moment, dividing one form of reality from another. "I took a bath this morning."

Mrs Mayhew shifted forward in her swivel-backed desk chair, impressing the flay of manila folders with her speckly, wattled elbows.

"Maybe it would do you good, young lady. Maybe you need to take off your clothes and climb into a nice hot bath. Then I could scrub you all over with the dishrag. Maybe we could use the dishrag to wipe that smug look off your face."

It took Sal a moment to decide how to deal with this one.

"Maybe tomorrow," Sal said.

"I don't think you heard me."

"I heard you just fine."

"Maybe I'm not asking your opinion. Maybe I'm telling you how things have to be, whether you like it or not."

Mrs Mayhew didn't sweat so much as precipitate a fine odorless mist around her eyes and ears. When she breathed, her nostrils flared, as if she couldn't get thoughts out of her mind fast enough.

"Maybe it's up to *me* to tell little girls whether they should take their baths or not," Mrs Mayhew continued. "Maybe these selfsame little girls should do what I tell them. And if they don't do what I tell them, maybe they should be punished. Maybe that would teach them a lesson about when to say yes and when to say no to a person who loves them. Especially when they're dealing with an important person like myself."

"Whatever you say, Grandma."

"Would you like me to call Tim in here?"

"I'd rather you didn't."

"Do you know what happens to bad little girls? Especially when they don't take baths like they're supposed to?"

Whenever Sal spoke with Mrs Mayhew, it felt like receding across a flat gray desert of sand and tumbling sagebrush. Mrs Mayhew's intensity was not an easy thing to live with, Sal thought. Which is probably why nobody talks to her but me.

"I wouldn't like that at all," Sal said.

Sometimes you won games simply because nobody else wanted to play. And a win is always better than a draw, Sal thought. Even in a game as pointless as this one.

"And when I don't like something, Mrs Mayhew, I go to bed and shut my eyes until morning. Because you'd be surprised, Mrs Mayhew, how fast things go away. Especially the ones I don't like."

———

Sal's room was bearable, despite its teddy-bear-flocked wallpaper, and a giraffe-shaped table lamp, which brooded over her single bed like a vulture. On a more positive side, the mattress and foam pillows were hard and unimpressible, just the way Sal liked them, and the flannel sheets had been worn into a soft blur of indefinition. If you closed your eyes, a room like this was perfect for contemplating everybody but yourself. It was only when Sal opened her eyes that things appeared tidy and discomfiting.

"Mrs Mayhew says say your prayers. But this isn't an order; it's more like a suggestion. If you feel the need for spiritual comfort, then saying your prayers may alleviate any inner distress or turmoil you're suffering. That's all she's trying to say."

The night-guardian was a gray-haired man named Mr Peterson, who wore an apron and a blue linen shirt with his name stitched over the breast. He often wiped his hands with a checkered tea towel that hung from his back pocket, as if winding himself up on a very small spring.

"The light switch is here. And there's a glass of water on the table. If you need anything in the night, just knock on the wall three times. I'm next door and will be over in a flash, wearing night-vision goggles and wielding a Louisville Slugger. We don't allow monsters under our beds, Stephanie, and if we find one? We make them wish they'd never been born."

Mr Peterson fulfilled the role of Mrs Mayhew's husband, only they slept in different rooms, never arrived or left anywhere together, and represented different philosophies of life.

Whenever Mrs Mayhew wasn't around, Mr Peterson was, and vice versa.

"I don't usually need anything in the night," Sal told him, closing her eyes against Mr Peterson's intensity. "And if I did need anything, I'd get it myself."

"If you want me, let me know – that's all I'm saying. Now, would you be requiring any help with your prayers? We are a non-denominational children's rescue service here at St John's, and while many of our guests say prayers to God or Jesus, just as many say their prayers to Buddha or Mohammed. Everybody needs faith in a Higher Power, Stephanie. Otherwise, they spend their lives believing in nothing. How about if I get started? Then, once you get the hang of it, you can carry on by yourself. Ready?"

Sal gripped the frayed hem of her flannel sheet.

"Okay," she said softly, closing her eyes. "I guess so."

Mr Peterson breathed heavily for a few moments. It was as if he needed to establish his presence inside the room before he could speak to anybody outside it.

Finally, Mr Peterson said, "Now I lay me down to sleep."

It felt dishonest praying to Higher Powers, Sal thought. But it was the only way to get rid of Mr Peterson.

"Now I lay me down to sleep."

"And abandon the illusion of materiality to explore a greater reality that surrounds me."

"The greatness that surrounds me."

"I walk without fear in the darkness."

"I'm not scared of the darkness."

"For I know that the Great Presence – you might want to insert the name of your preferred Higher Power here, Stephanie, such as God, or Jesus, etcetera – will always be there to protect and guide me towards true spiritual perfection. Or whatever."

"Spiritual perfection," Sal said. "And so forth."

Sal couldn't wait any longer. She opened her eyes.

Mr Peterson was looking at her.
It was a long time to look at somebody.
But that was Mr Peterson's choice.

———————

They referred to the act of "giving a deposition" as a "painless process" which wouldn't involve any form of disclosure that Sal didn't want to make. If she felt uncomfortable at any time, they would deactivate the video recorder, disassemble the white partition backdrop, and put an end to things. If she asked to return to the Safe House, they would take her. If she found any subject awkward or unpleasant, they would move on to something else. In fact, she didn't have to say anything if she didn't want to: she could just nod or shake her head, or roll her eyes, or shrug her shoulders. Trained professionals could interpret what she meant – however clearly (or not) she chose to express it.

"The main thing to remember, Stephanie, is that you'll never have to see either of those dreadful people ever again," the Deputy District Attorney promised. He was a cheaply-scented man with badly trimmed fingernails and an expensive, soundless gold watch. "When you look at them through this special one-way glass, they can't see you; you can only see them. Nobody will know your name or where you live. Worse comes to worst, you'll enter witness protection, and we'll send you to live in a different state, where you'll receive a monthly stipend, even after you finish college. And college, by the way, will be the most important decision you ever make. Before I went to college, I was just some loser kid with bad acne who couldn't get a date for the senior prom, but now look at me. I'm Deputy District Attorney for one of the ten most populous states in the union. And if you don't think *that's* improved my love life, well. You don't know state politics."

It was like hiding on the wrong side of somebody else's dream. Sal was presented with a cold can of Fruit Surprise and a soft canvas deck chair; then she was placed in front of a dirty window, speckled with small white bits of what resembled organic matter, as if somebody had been flossing in front of it. Then, on the other side of the glass, a door opened in one of the pale walls, and Tim helped Grandma into the room. Grandma shuffled a few steps at a time, grasping Tim's arm through his red flannel shirt, and emitting long vowel-rich Grandma-sounds. Under his left arm, Tim carried Grandma's aluminum walker.

"Just a few more steps," Tim said encouragingly. His voice was buzzy with static, like a poorly-tuned transistor radio. He led Grandma towards two matching wooden chairs with white vinyl seats that were waiting in the middle of the room like a test. Two boxes – tick one. Don't tick both boxes or you'll be disqualified.

"Don't be scared, Grandma. Once we've answered a few questions, they'll send us home. I'll fix you fresh peaches and cream and a sandwich with Deviled Ham."

Meanwhile, on Sal's side of the glass, the Deputy District Attorney activated the video camera on a tripod, and marked down the time and date on a white sheet. At the top, in bold black letters, the sheet said:

Formal Declaration – Child

What else would it say? Sal thought.

"Do you recognize these people?" he asked.

It took Sal a moment to realize he was speaking to her.

"It's Grandma and Tim," she said.

"Would you like to tell me anything about Grandma and Tim?"

Sal thought again.

"Not really," she said.

"That Grandma is certainly a strange-looking old lady, don't you think? What do you think about this so-called Grandma? Was she nice to you? Did she promise you things, like sweets or toys. Or even little dollies?"

Tim was helping Grandma into the chair on the left. Then he took the one on the right.

Uh-oh, Sal thought. Tests are always unfair – unless you're the one giving them.

"I don't like dollies," Sal said finally.

The Deputy District Attorney adjusted himself in his seat until he faced Sal. "What don't you like about dollies, Stephanie? Would you please explain?"

It was the only answer Sal had given him that she didn't have to think about.

"They're tiny," she said. "And helpless. They look at you with those empty eyes that don't have anything interesting to say. They want you to talk to them, and cuddle them, and give them baths in the sink, but they never give anything back. They're whiny and useless and don't care about anybody but themselves. They don't really care about you. They just want you to care about them."

"They'll be wearing ankle bracelets and undergoing twenty-four hour satellite surveillance when I'm through," the Deputy District Attorney assured Sal later that day, walking her out to Mrs Mayhew in the waiting room. "They won't be able to apply for a job in this country, or a goddamn Mastercard, without everybody receiving three copies of your anonymous deposition. If they go jogging through a neighborhood they're not supposed to be in, the dogs'll bark, and patrol cars will pick them up on their sonar. Which is to say you've been a terrific help, little lady. I know it must have been painful, digging up old terrors. But for every moment of discomfort, you've saved several young lives from the humiliation that you endured at the hands of those, pardon my French, bastards. Now, I'm going to turn you over to the highly capable Mrs Mayhew, and she's going to drive you back to your shelter. Perhaps we'll meet again, little lady, or perhaps we won't. But I'll remember you in my prayers. And I'll pray that you eventually find your way home to your true, loving parents again. Unless, of course, they turn out to be the ones who initiated you into this world of serial child-victimization in the first place. And then, of course, I'll pray that you never see them again."

It was hard for Sal to recall what she had done to deserve so much praise. The Deputy District Attorney had read a series of monotone questions to her from a thick, leather-bound folder, and she had replied affirmatively whenever possible. When it wasn't possible, she simply averted her eyes while the Deputy District Attorney performed a sequence of verbal gymnastics.

"The interviewee is not replying," he said, leaning into the whirring video camera, which perched atop the gleaming chrome-and-black-metal tripod like a robotic bird. "Will the interviewee nod or shake her head in order to clarify? She will not. Will the interviewee give me some signal if we're on the right track? Let it be noted that she has glanced into my eyes. It is eleven-fourteen a.m. Did you glance into my eyes, little girl? Can I take your glance as an affirmative? Let it be noted that she has glanced into my eyes for a third time. I would regard this as significant eye-contact. It is eye-contact designed to convey significance. So let's take this as a possible-affirmative and move on."

On the ride back to the shelter, Mrs Mayhew floated beside Sal in a tranquil doze of recollection. Through her bluish, thickly-mascaraed lashes, the entire world must have appeared as bright and sunny as some magical kingdom in one of the Saturday morning cartoon programs Sal dreaded like crowded elevators, or stomach flu. She steadily rotated the steering wheel back and forth, as if she were navigating through soft white clouds, and never looked once at the rear-view mirror, even though Sal was sitting directly behind her in the back seat.

"The greatest beauty of children, Stephanie, is their supreme resiliency," Mrs Mayhew explained as she drove. "But sometimes, this resiliency is like a big soft curtain of unreality which prevents them from learning how to deal with bad people. Children have no sense of right or wrong; they have no sense of injustice. They only have three ideas about how the world operates, and those three ideas can be summarized as negation, acceptance, and control. That's why the child's first word is usually *no*. As in, 'No, I don't want any apple juice.' Or, 'No, I don't want to go to bed.' Or, 'No, I don't want to be ritually humiliated by Satanists in a dark room with too many candles.' For children, *no* is this super-powerful word that can be used to control a world that wants to control them. It's the most beautiful notion of hegemony and power that the child will ever know."

They were driving down the sort of streets Sal had seen a thousand times before. Bars and Laundromats with broken marquees, thrift shops and bridal shops and convenience stores and something concrete, boarded-over, and monolithic that might once have been either a post office or a bank. Stores and buildings and mean-slatted houses filled with things and categories of things, accumulations of objects that lay buried deep in their own shadows like thinking machines, or hidden implications. I've been in a house like that one, Sal thought mildly, drawn through the passing sequence of buildings like a machinery-manufactured widget on a conveyor belt. I've been in a house like that one, and a Laundromat like that one, and even a restaurant like that one. But I've never been in a house like that one, or this one over here. It might be interesting being in a house like that one. Or maybe, after all is said and done, it wouldn't be interesting at all.

"Eventually, the word *no* just doesn't cut it anymore. Children develop; they learn to speak, plan, strategize, and grab. They think about the meaning of words, and make them complicated, until they aren't even words anymore. They learn to say yes when they mean no, and maybe when they mean yes, and so on and so forth. They learn to dissemble. And once they've learned to dissemble, Stephanie, they can never be children again. They are cut off from the genuine meaning of their lives. They become conspirators in their own subjugation."

Mrs Mayhew was smoking a long filter-tip cigarette and flicking ashes out the half-cocked side window, driving and smiling as if she knew exactly where she wanted to go. "In my profession, we call this the meaning-formation stage of child development. A period of growth when the mind over-reaches its spatial limitations, and tests the limits of immaterial properties. I know I haven't discussed these dimensions of childhood previously, Stephanie, but you have to understand that for a while I didn't think you were ready to address them. Until, of course, I read that deposition you helped Ron prepare. And once I read that deposition, I knew you were ready to understand anything."

They seemed to view and review the same streets in no particular order, the same buildings and imitations of buildings, as if they were trapped in the rotations of some circular landscape, affixed to perspective like a nail hammered into a cylinder of wood. I've been here before, Sal thought to herself, motionless in the steady surge of Mrs Mayhew's voice. I've been here, I've been here, I've even been here. And if Mrs Mayhew gets her way, I'll have to keep coming here again and again. It's not because Mrs Mayhew is cruel or anything. She just lacks any form of imagination.

Mrs Mayhew's voice compared Sal to asteroids, solar systems, tidal geography, and veins of ore buried in underground caverns. She compared her to sequences of numbers in an open set, a roving spiritual demi-urge, and a memory of water. It was like taking a ride through a series of ideas, Sal thought. Mrs Mayhew's car wasn't a mode of transportation anymore. It was an always-developing opportunity for understanding Sal.

"I had to keep a lot of things under my hat," Mrs Mayhew confessed after an hour or so. They had looped outward from one cloverleaf exchange to another until they seemed to be pursuing every direction at once. "But the fact of the matter, Stephanie, is that we're never going to find your parents. That's because you weren't produced by normal biological procedures. Your mommy is the earth and your daddy is the sky, and you were condensed into existence, like rain or enlightenment. For many years, Stephanie, I have belonged to a secret society known as the Shapers, who have waited countless millennia for the arrival of a little girl exactly like you. A little girl who will condemn the sinners to eternal damnation and suffering. And when I say sinners, Stephanie, I think you know the sort of sinners I'm talking about. The ones who prey on little girls and little boys. The ones who conspire to obstruct people like me from doing good work. Because when you get right down to it, Stephanie, there are only two types of people in this world. Those who want to preserve children and make them happy, and share in their miraculous freshness of spirit. And those who want to corrupt and defoul them, and turn every child they meet into someone as filthy, dishonest, and irredeemable as themselves."

It was as if everybody had known about Sal's special status all along. They were just waiting for the right time to tell her.

"For someone like you," Mr Peterson explained later that night in Sal's hard, imperishable room with its 3-D framed portraits of Jesus, Buddha, and Mohammed on the walls, "prayer isn't a means of communicating with God. It's a means of expressing Universal Harmony in the eternal now-ness, which is why I've emphasized abstract prayer so much at bedtime. I know you're a private person, Stephanie, but many of us await your guidance. There's Fred in the kitchen, and Sally who does the cleaning. There's the Deputy District Attorney, and most of the primary case-workers at the State Board of Child Protection – except maybe Alice, who's a bit too Pope-obsessed, if you ask me. Those of us who are genuinely devoted to the cause of children can find each other in crowds; we come together in coffee shops and restaurants, and organize web-chats on the internet, and book clubs at Borders, where news of your arrival has spread like wildfire. You are known as The Girl of Many Names. You are known as the Pre-Celestial Incarnation. In most religions there is a savior who releases souls from bondage, and a destroyer who immolates the wicked, and I don't have to tell you which of these creatures is sitting with me right now, just about to say her bedtime prayers and weave the people of our world into a book of common devotion."

It had been what adults referred to as a "long day," stretching from one pole of experience to the other, like one of those arcing lines on a global map that keeps going until it rejoins itself. So much space to get lost in, Sal thought. No wonder I'm thirsty and need a glass of water.

"First your prayers, Stephanie," Mr Peterson said simply. "Say your prayers like a good little girl and I'll get you that water."

Mr Peterson got down on his knees and leaned his elbows into the edge of Sal's hard bed. Meanwhile, Sal sat up against her pillows and looked at the bald spot on the back of his head. It was mottled with thick ink-stain-like freckles. It resembled a stellar chart of the universe in formation, expanding patterns of furious elemental matter.

"Now I lay myself in the arms of the world," Mr Peterson said.

Sal thought about the back of Mr Peterson's head for

a moment. Then she said softly, "I sleep in the arms of the world."

"And seek redemption in the eyes of everybody I left behind."

"Everybody I left behind."

"I will triumph in the night."

"Triumph in the night."

"And find my way back to the planet which expelled me."

"The place I used to be."

"I'll cross mountains and oceans as a disembodied being."

"Mountains and oceans."

"And cleanse the world of bad creatures in an avalanche of fire."

"Destroy and make them mine."

Mr Peterson waddled his elbows forward a few steps across the mattress. One freckled hand passed across his bald spot, performed a brief eclipse, and disappeared into the dark folds of his body.

"I will bless those who saved me. I will recall them and make them vigilant. I will open the eyes of people who can't see. I will inhabit their cities and make them mine."

Sal was thinking about water. She hoped it would arrive in a tall clear glass. Water didn't taste right in a hard-plastic container, especially one that was scratched and pocked from a thousand fingernails.

"I guess I should say their names now. Is that what I'm supposed to do?"

Mr Peterson did not lift his forehead from the mattress. He had given her all the help he could.

Sal sighed. It was the closest she ever came to crying.

"Then I bless Daddy, who found me and carried me away."

"God bless the Father."

"And Mommy, who taught me things I remember more than her."

"And the eternal Earth Mother."

"And I bless young people in new houses, and everybody in Laundromats, and the Unhappy Man who never met me, and all the people who watched me pass by."

"And all unhappy men as they pass from this earth."

This can't go on much longer, Sal consoled herself. I'm running out of ideas.

"And finally, I bless Tim and Grandma, for all the things I said about them that may or may not be true. And you, Mr Peterson. And Mrs Mayhew. I hope you both find as much happiness as I did, though I think that's unlikely. Because happiness isn't about who you are or what you own, Mr Peterson. Happiness is about all the people you leave behind."

———

Mr Peterson was snoring by the time Sal lifted up her blankets and pulled her legs gently from underneath his clasped hands and the slow blue pulse of his neck. The beige pile carpet muffled the sound of her footsteps. She walked to the door and looked into the hall.

For the first time, Sal became aware of other children out there, residing secretly like mice in the walls. Children behind other doors, sleeping in other beds. Children who couldn't find their mommies and daddies, or who had been taken away from their mommies and daddies, or who didn't want to have anything to do with their mommies and daddies, on account of questionable physical relationships, or faulty child-guardian behavior patterns. Some of these children had learned to tuck themselves into bed at night. They found comfort in dollies, plastic dinosaurs, favorite pillows, and softly textured blankets. Others fell asleep staring at multicultural religious portraits on the walls, or listening to classical music on portable cd players. None of them knew Sal's name, or had seen any of the things

Sal had seen. They weren't very interesting. They definitely belonged alone in their rooms.

"She brings us love and guidance," whispered the voice of a young boy behind one of the doors. "If we're good, she'll take us with her. If we're bad, she may never leave."

Sal stepped barefoot across the carpet. In the Central Living Arena (as Mr Peterson referred to it) brand new matching block-shaped furniture sat empty and waiting. Angular and meaningful, Sal thought. The sort of furniture that doesn't let you get too comfortable.

She found Matron Alice in the storage room ironing white smocks and off-white cotton dresses and humming something Sal recognized from the radio.

"Gonna love me when she comes," Matron Alice whispered. "Gonna love me all night long. Gonna love me when she comes. Make me love her all night long." Matron Alice was smiling and happy. She didn't look up.

"What can we do for you, Miss Stephanie? Have you come to share your eternal wisdom with Matron Alice? Or perhaps you'd like me to make you a cheese sandwich, or a strawberry-flavored Pop Tart for your midnight snack." The humming noise continued to emanate from Matron Alice even while she spoke. It was like a gentle subterranean whisper. A slow shift of intention in the night.

Sal sort of liked Matron Alice. But that didn't mean she was going to tell her anything she didn't have to.

"I'm not looking for sandwiches or Pop Tarts," Sal said. "I just thought I'd come down and get my old pink dress, the one I used to wear. Mr Peterson said it was okay. He said nothing should be kept secret from me anymore."

THE LOVING OF DADDY

When Sal walked out into the wide, freshly-demarcated parking lot, she found Daddy sitting at the steering wheel of his white van doing a crossword puzzle and chewing a wad of colorless gum. It's funny how things happen, Sal thought. You expect them to happen and then they do.

"You weren't the hardest person in the world to track down," Daddy said, folding his crossword puzzle into a metal doorside pocket that resembled the whorled inner chambers of a nautilus. Then, shifting against his brown-beaded ergonomic backrest, he cranked on the scratchy engine with his jangly assortment of keys and plastic lucky charms. The engine revved, revved again, and after a broken shudder, caught and thundered through a greasy cloud of burning oil and pent-up emissions as Daddy locomoted slowly through the dark streets like a slowly waking mechanical ox, pursued by the thwipping, echoing beat of road dividers, finding his way back into the past that was finally Sal's again.

"I couldn't buy a carton of milk or open a newspaper without seeing your picture, or reading your vital statistics. There I'd be, eating my sandwich, and staring at your photo on "Hard Copy," "Lost and Loved," or "The Six O'Clock News, with Katie Couric." For a while, you were hotter than sliced bread; you were getting more air-time than J Lo. At first, I thought I shouldn't bother you anymore; I should let you live your new life as Stephanie or Sally or whatever you were calling yourself and stay out of your way. Maybe I'd done enough damage.

Maybe you didn't want to see me again, or you'd forgotten how much we meant to each other. But then the weirder stories started coming through. Mysterious girl delivered to hospital by Secret Sex Abuse Network. Amnesia orphan awakens from coma to testify against Child-Sacrifice Cult. As I understood, these characters who dropped you off at the hospital were linked to the Mafia, the State Board of Education, and several local nursery and elementary schools that couldn't be named for legal reasons. Some underground organization was selling children to drug cartels, Satanic death-worshippers, and a Pope-sanctioned cabal of discredited Catholic priests. And whenever you see Catholic priests linked to kids in the national media, Sal, you know it's not all horses and buggies. They kept calling you Stephanie Hardwick, possibly from California, could anyone identify you, and I figured it must be my little Sal, trying to save her fair name from all this public brouhaha, who could blame her. After all, that was one kid who knew how to keep a secret. It made me remember how thoughtlessly I abandoned you to that evil old Mrs Whats-her-name, the old witch in the bungalow complex, you remember. My emotions haven't been easy to live with since then, Sal. I just kept thinking how I promised to be a perfect daddy and how long did I manage? Three weeks, maybe four. I owed you another try. Or maybe I owed it to myself – who knows?"

The van smelled different, Sal thought, and so did Daddy. It was as if the dimensions of this cluttered space had been taken apart and put back together with several small pieces missing. Something was wrong. But Sal couldn't put her finger on it.

"I told them you'd come back," Sal said after a while. She had already strapped herself securely into the broken-backed passenger seat with the familiar gray harness; she was looking at a hole in the dashboard where the cigarette lighter used to be. "They said they were looking for you, and I should tell them everything, like your driver's license number, or your social security number, or any of those other numbers you keep in your wallet. But I wouldn't tell them because I knew you'd find me. I had to be patient. Things would get better in the long run. Eventually you'd find me again and take me home."

He wasn't the same Daddy anymore; he tried to pretend he was the same Daddy, but he couldn't fool Sal. For one thing, he had quit smoking and taken up chewing large gray wads of Nicorette gum, which he left lying around in speckless glass motel ashtrays like some basic half-formed immutable stuff. He didn't like V8 juice anymore, or taking long morning excursions into the bathroom, or encouraging Sal to play alone in her room. He didn't even wear jeans and torn tennis shoes – only thick-corded casual slacks and high-top leather-laced workboots.

"None of us wanted to see you hook up with social services," Daddy told her a few days later, when they arrived at his unfurnished ranch-style home with a two car garage in a fifties-style flatland of countless other open-plan ranch homes with two car garages. "But now that they've picked us up on their child-abuse radar, we'll have to keep on our toes. The house has a decent yard, and when the weather improves, maybe I can build a play area, or a swingset and slide. I'll take care of the shopping, and run any errands that need running, and you can stay home and mind the store. There's no point taking chances. Like just one of those storefront minicams picks you up and we're through. I'll be neutered, lobotomized, and working the chain gang with Father Junipero Serra and that lot. And if I even *think* about talking to a kid, or asking her name, or feeling any paternal affection for her whatsoever, I'll start vomiting gruel, like that poor bastard in *A Clockwork Orange*." Daddy pulled into a wide driveway that was stained with oil, like one of Mrs Mayhew's ink blots. The best part about ink blots, Sal thought, is that they always mean exactly what you want them to.

(I see a man in a cave, Sal had told Mrs Mayhew. He hasn't any money, and he hasn't any friends. He figures he might as well stay in his cave. He's not happy, but he can't think of anywhere else he'd rather be.)

Daddy went around to the back of the van and unloaded two cardboard boxes filled with damp, mossy wood and kindling. Then he escorted Sal through an alley carpeted with soggy, wind-flung newspapers until they reached the back gate, which leaned cockeyed on a broken yellow hinge. Sal could walk through the crooked opening without touching the gate, or unlatching the door. She didn't know if this was a good quality when it came to backyard gates, or a bad one.

The weeds back here were taller than Sal, bristling with thorns and weirdly serrated, miniaturized beast-like heads. Little broken paths had been trampled into them, where islands of flagstone and cinder block lay distributed at strange angles like Druidic markers, smelling of peat moss and slugs. Wading through this spiny bearded jungle, they reached a twisted brick patio, where smaller, thornier weeds emerged from cracks and fissures to form wispy, scraggly lines and curlicues, like arcane notations on a sheet of paper Sal might find fluttering across a parking lot. In the middle of the patio, a sagging cardboard box stood upside down, propped up by its torn brown flaps like something octopoidal just emerged from the sea. On top of the box, two green plastic plates were laid beside disposable cafeteria-style cutlery, a pair of dew-soggy napkins, and a dead rose.

"It's not much, I'll admit. But it's off the social map, and that's what we're looking for. Not registered for the electoral rolls, mailmen don't deliver, and nobody comes by to check the meters. So let's grin and bear it for a while, even if you can't go to school right away. I'm sure there're a few things left I can teach you – though I can't quite think what those things might be. Here, open that picture window – pull harder, it's a little rusty

– and help me unload these boxes. Then, if she's up, you can go down the hall and introduce yourself to your baby sister. She's really excited to meet you. Last time I saw her, all she talked about was you."

———————

She was like a gray smudge of newsprint, or something formed from twiggy garden clay. Her smell lifted from the warped floor-bound mattress before she did, huddled in her depression of muggy blankets and grimy stuffed toys. You can't fool me, Sal thought, standing over the mattress in a small bedroom at the end of a long hallway. There were water stains on all the walls, as if the floods of Daddy's first disappearance had ebbed from this place too, taking with them everything but Daddy.

She had blonde hair, the sort Sal often imagined for herself, ringleted, copperish, tangled into oily blobs and mottled by a substance that resembled chewing gum or molten wax. Her stuffed toys were just the sort that Sal hated. Teddy bears and white seal cubs and giraffes, gray stuffing protruding where their limbs used to be. Their ears had been chewed until they resembled pulpy termite-eaten wood, and many of the buttons demarcating eyes and nostrils had fallen off, lending their expressions attitudes of surprise, bemusement, and despair that hadn't been earned. Without pride or forbearance, they lay assembled around the little sister like the vestiges of some retreating army.

"He claims you're my sister," Sal said, standing over the bed where the little girl didn't move or turn her head or manifest any degree of volition or concern. "But you're not really my sister, so get used to it. The basic fact of the matter is that I'm older than you are, so I make the rules, and my rules are simple. I don't like to talk and I don't like to listen. And Daddy's my daddy, not yours, though I don't mind if you talk with him, or play with him, since I'm not possessive. I just like to be clear about things, especially definitions. Which is to say that I mind very much if you even *think* about taking my seat in the van, or drinking juice from my glass, or eating food from my plate. I don't like germs, or other people's skin particles getting into my food, but otherwise I'm pretty easy to live with. I believe in live and let live. I believe in the Golden Rule."

The little girl was too motionless and unresponsive to seem natural. She's probably not very bright, Sal reflected. I could teach her a thing or two.

"How are you kids doing back there!" Daddy shouted from the other room. He was making a series of loud, sudden noises, as if he were kicking an empty cardboard box from one end of the house to the other. "When you're hungry, I'll order pizza. What do you want on your pizza? Pepperoni or plain cheese?"

Sal turned and looked at the door, which was warped and moldy around the hinges. She hadn't noticed the smell of damp until now.

"Plain cheese, Daddy," she said.

When she looked back down at the mattress, the little sister was lying on her back in her pool of blankets, her eyes wide open and staring at Sal from a weird angle, as if her neck was broken.

"What about your little sister, Sal? What does *she* want on her pizza?"

But people can get used to anything, Sal consoled herself. Especially when they're little.

She could smell the pizza already.

"Plain cheese is fine with her also," Sal said, more softly this time. "She says that whatever's okay with me is okay with her, too."

She wasn't like a little sister; she was more like the emergence of Sal's voice from the deepest structure of Sal. She was like digging through a tunnel of words into a place where words didn't matter.

"Life is little more than a series of opportunities for self-improvement," Sal explained. They were sitting on inverted blue plastic milk crates on the back patio, pretending to sip tea from paper cups at the cardboard table. The sun was a high haze of density and irreflection. There didn't seem to be anybody else alive in the entire world. "And you can either take advantage of these opportunities or pass them by. New experiences, for example. Or new people. You learn from everything that happens to you in this life, and from everybody you meet, and then you take what you learn, and put it to good use by building a stronger notion of who you are, and where you want to go. Sometimes, you stay with other people for a while, or they stay with you. You work together like a single individual, and this is called a family, or a business enterprise, or a corporation, especially if it offers stock options or medical insurance, things like that. But most of the time, and this is the saddest fact of life I know, we only make progress in our personal journey at the expense of other people. If they get in our way, we have to walk past them and pretend we didn't notice. And if we get in their way, they have to do the same to us. It's not cruelty that causes us to act this way. It's evolution. It's how people improve across space and time."

Sal's baby sister didn't even look like Sal, that was the funny part. She didn't look like Daddy, or Mrs Mayhew, or any of the people children normally looked like; come to think of it, she didn't even look like herself, from one day to another. Some days her hair was dark with a reddish tinge; other days, it was reddish with a dark tinge, or dirty blonde, or even gray in places, especially when she had just finished washing it with rusty water from the kitchen tap. Her eyes were colorless and vapid, concerned with nothing but themselves. The tea cups didn't even have real tea in them, just muddy water from the rain gutter. They didn't even match.

"For example," Sal continued, refusing to give up on the little girl the same way Daddy had once given up on her, "when you're born, you have a mommy and daddy, and they both love you very much, or so they pretend. They feed you, and educate you, and provide you with clothes and play-things until you're old enough to leave. Then you *do* leave, but you carry their memory with you always, even when you don't know it. You find yourself saying things you heard them say. You start imitating their gestures. And eventually, in a funny way you hardly even notice, you start to become them, in a series of informal, disconnected little actions, as if they're emerging from your body, and not the other way around. As life goes on, you can't leave them behind, however hard you try. Even when you've forgotten what they look like, they're always with you. It's like stringing beads on a necklace, these moments of behavior that keep emerging from you, like this idea I once had about dust on the moon. You see, the moon is constantly attracting tiny particles of dust drifting in from all over the universe. Everything that doesn't belong anywhere else, see. Somehow it all ends up on the moon."

The words that arose in Sal now were like streams of thought and meaning that had been running secretly through Sal's body since the day she learned to leave people behind. Particles of language that felt continuous and intact, spilling from the lumpy surfeit of Sal, a steady state of always developing knowledge as constant as rain, or patterns of landscape. Sitting at the table, Sal watched the little sister pretend to pour pretend tea from a sour-stained pint-sized milk bottle into her muddy tea cups. It was as if she were pretending not to hear Sal talk. Or maybe she was just a slow listener.

"Would you like sugar with your tea?" the little girl asked. The smudge and tangle of her features seemed to move around her face, like industrial stirring mechanisms in a deep vat of chocolate, or the red-eyed storm of Jupiter. Insubstantiality was the most implacable thing about her. It was certainly the only thing about her that Sal could bring herself to like.

"No, thank you," Sal said simply. "I never take sugar in my tea. That's because sugar's for kids who never figure out what's really going on."

———

"I was once a lot like you," Sal explained, tucking the little sister into her muddle of blankets each night. Whenever Daddy was off finding things to bring home in his van, Sal would prepare the evening meals – packaged sandwich meats, sliced white bread, and rusty red apples – and perform the soft rituals of bedtime. "I hadn't achieved form or resolution yet. I didn't know what I wanted from life, or what life wanted from me. I just lay around like this passive object, letting myself be lifted from one cushion of warmth to another, sucking on anything I could get my hands on. Fingers, nipples, soft plastic hoops, pencils, you name it. I had about as much ambition as a stuffed animal, residing wherever I happened to be. Then, as I developed dexterity, I learned to hold things with my fingers; I rolled, I crawled; I achieved things that previously seemed beyond my grasp. I extended my thoughts into other rooms and spaces, until eventually I got lost in them. Somebody else's yard or driveway. A foreign food aisle in some huge supermarket. Indefinite acres of grass and dirt, and the strange regions that develop between buildings. Certain people lived in this building, and other people lived in that one, and once I managed this basic conceptual leap, I graduated into other concepts of distance entirely. The spaces between planets, for instance. Or the ones inside my own head. I learned to recognize these spaces for what they were. The regions where meaning happens. The only places worth being at all."

The little sister had a way of listening without paying attention, retreating into her shapelessness like an amphibian into the muck. Whoever came up with the idea of evolution, Sal thought, never spent any time with this kid.

"I used to imagine things," the little sister said, her eyes slowly closing. "People who played with me. People who lived in different houses, people with different names. But now I can't imagine anyone but Daddy."

Daddy would be gone for days sometimes, leaving behind a few canned goods, or a bottle of stale water on the kitchen counter, and a sense of privilege that Sal had never experienced before. She could go anywhere she wanted within a confined series of choices, and there was nobody waiting to tell her what to do when she got there. Many of the rooms and closets were occupied by spiders of every possible shape and size, spinning geometric webs like commerce, entrapping blackish lumps of bugs that continued squirming until fate found them. Other rooms were occupied by broken furniture, sacks of concrete and peat moss. But the best places of all were the places that nobody but Sal ever visited, such as the hard rat-scrabbled maze of wooden crates in the attic, or the flooded immensity of basement where Sal would sometimes descend to taste the milky water with a plastic spoon.

Usually she waited until well after the little sister was asleep before opening the crooked wooden door. She wasn't sure who she was afraid of disturbing: the scummy surface of water, or the smell of her own body reflected by the bare-beamed walls and cracked plaster ceiling. It was almost as if the only person she might disturb down here was herself.

"I've never heard the sound of my own voice so clearly before," Sal whispered, approaching the flooded concrete floors and the hard emergent shapes of the leaning boiler, the deflated power mower, and the dissolving stuffed chairs, their ragged flowers of dye blossoming like pollen or seaweed. "When nobody else is around, my voice sounds like this. I speak words like these. And when I cover my mouth, I sound like this." Sal would crouch on the bottom step and look around at the swampy enclosed basement, the blackly curtained single slotted window through which a bit of moonlight gleamed without illuminating anything, and recall the history of her life that was rapidly disappearing. The things that had happened before she had words to describe them. The people she had met before she could tell anybody what they said. "If it hadn't been for Daddy, I'd have lost everything," she whispered. "I wouldn't know where I came from, or where I've been. I wouldn't even remember all the nice people I met along the way."

In the morning, sometimes without having slept at all, Sal would open cans with a hammer and a blunt screwdriver, doling out their contents on fresh white paper plates which Daddy brought home in large plastic sacks from army surplus auctions, yard sales, and club-bound retail outlets. Pork and beans, stewed tomatoes, mandarin oranges in syrup, creamed spinach, pickled artichoke hearts, corned beef, and Deviled Ham. "The most important thing to remember," Sal reminded the little girl at every meal, "is to diversify your diet, stay away from too much sugar and preservatives, and eat as much roughage as possible. Otherwise, you develop hyperactive social disorders, or diseases such as bowel cancer, hair loss, pimples, or even something called rickets, which usually only happens to sailors."

Talking to the little sister, Sal thought, was a lot like talking to yourself. You could tell her everything, and nobody could hold it against you the next morning.

If it wasn't raining, Sal took her little sister on long walks into the furthest extremes of the neighborhood. She couldn't seem to understand anything unless Sal showed her.

"Our neighborhood," Sal explained, holding the little girl's hand as if she were communicating by means of electrical impulses, "isn't as nice as this one, but that's nothing to be ashamed about. Just look around you: nicer houses, nicer cars, nicer yards, nicer flowerbeds, nicer everything. People take care of their possessions out here, while back in our neck of the woods, they let things go to pot. But I don't want you thinking that one neighborhood's better than any other neighborhood. In fact, they're all pretty much the same. People live in houses. They go to work and raise children. They drive cars. They don't look one another in the eye. And if you're a kid, it doesn't matter if your neighborhood is a nice one, or a not-so-nice one, or some weird borderland in-between, because you're never allowed to go anywhere by yourself, unless you're being escorted by your parents or their appointed representatives. Daddy says it wasn't always this way. It used to be that kids ran around to their heart's content. But it's definitely how kids live today, constantly being monitored and tended, exercised and educated until they're as docile as sheep. Only they don't produce anything useful, like wool or lamb chops. They just shuffle along, doing what they're told, thinking what they're supposed to. They never surprise you. They're always the same as everybody else."

The little sister was so unenthusiastic that she often depressed Sal. In fact, the only thing the little girl liked about going for walks was returning home again.

"I'm tired," the little girl would say whenever Sal finished telling her something important, or showing her a formidable-looking, gray-walled institution worth avoiding, such as the local elementary school, or a franchise family restaurant. "I'm hungry. I don't like it around here. I want to go home." She didn't resist Sal's momentum so much as exert a sort of spiritual friction. Her reluctance was like mass; it slowed everything down, even Sal.

"Exercise is important," Sal explained – to herself as much

as to the little sister. "So is fresh air and sunshine. You can't hide in the house all day, playing with your tea cups. Open the door, step outside. Find out what's going on. Nobody will tell you what's out there. It's something you've got to see for yourself."

———————

Often they returned well past dark to find Daddy sleeping in his white van, arms folded across the black steering wheel as if he were praying. Usually he parked two or three houses away, and when the little sister insisted on seeing Daddy for herself, Sal clutched her around the chest, as if she were performing the Heimlich maneuver, and lifted her high enough to see over the rubber-sealed verge of the driver-side window.

"That's Daddy sleeping," Sal said. "He's not dead or anything. He just needs his rest if he wants to come home and be a good daddy again."

Then Sal put the little sister down. It was like trying to amuse a sack of cement.

Daddy's tinnily resounding snores followed them through the alley and into the ruined backyard. They even infiltrated Sal's dreams, rough-sawn and metrically sustained, accompanied by images of large smog-breathing metal monsters on trolleys. When Daddy was nearby, it was almost the same as when he wasn't there. You could imagine him skimming across the world's surface on a current of air, observing things that looked like other things, experiencing events that had never happened to anybody but him.

"Sometimes us grownups have to stand back and let our children grow up by themselves," Daddy told them on one of those rare evenings when they ate dinner together. He would throw a blanket on the floor and they would pretend they were on a night-time picnic, swatting absently at beetles and grubs that emerged from the ruined carpets, passing around processed food in metal cans. "Maybe that's what I wanted to teach you on the day we first met, Sal. That you can't rely on anybody but yourself to be happy. I remember that first time we met very vividly, don't you? It was like falling in love or winning the lottery. I was in the basement fixing your boiler and you came in from the backyard with a popsicle stick. There wasn't any popsicle left, you were just chewing the splintery end of a piece of wood. You were wearing the same pink dress and those same pink shoes you're wearing now. And it was clear from your first glance that you didn't need me or anybody else to be who you already were. You didn't need those useless, cloying parents of yours, following you around with vials of cherry-flavored cough syrup and medicated ointment. You didn't need those stupid cartoons on the television, or the stuffed toys that littered your room, or even the roof over your head. You just needed that splintery, well-chewed little popsicle stick. I knew who you were the first moment I saw you. Which was the same moment I knew that we were meant to be together."

It was only a matter of time, Sal convinced herself. The trick was to make time stop mattering, and indulge yourself in as many pointless routines as possible.

"We need to write a book," Sal explained to the little girl one morning over stale sweet-rolls and orange juice. "And it has to be a good book or nobody will read it. In this book, we need to record the identities of everybody I've ever touched, or seen, or been in the same room with – even for a few minutes. They don't have to be important people; they just have to be memorable, with unique features that distinguish them from everybody else. For example, I often think about Tim and Grandma, and the time I had dinner in their home. Or the woman with the long blonde hair who let me sleep on a sofa next to her bed. I think about the men in large eighteen-wheel trucks who fed me in diners and gas stations, and old ladies who slept with their cats, and a large overweight man with bad breath who wouldn't let me inside his house because he was afraid of burglars, so he made me sleep in the garage on an aluminum cot. It was a really nice garage, by the way. Really large and cool, and filled with boxes of interesting things. This book shouldn't just be about people, but about the things they're attached to, which are often the most interesting things about them. Like their jewelry, or their furniture, or the framed photos on their bureaus, or their cars, or the various rooms and closets in their houses. Most people don't exist outside the things they own; don't ask me why, they just don't. It's almost as if the things own *them*, and not the other way around."

The best part about the little sister, Sal often thought, was that she never paid attention to the world, which made her a perfect collaborator. When Sal talked, she listened. When Sal moved or gestured, she followed Sal with her eyes. When Sal sat beside her, she grew less animated, like a computer on Standby. But when Sal left the room, a restless intensity developed in her limbs; she fidgeted, hummed out loud, and refused to betray any indication of anxiety or duress. She was never happy, and never unhappy. She was simply with Sal, or not with Sal, and her body strained against these two ranges of existence, like a rabbit skin on a wooden frame, drying in the sun. She had nothing to offer but the reflective surface of herself. And for Sal, that was enough.

"Some day, they'll ask you to remember everything about me," Sal assured the little sister, on an evening when they sat before the picture window and gazed out at the ruined backyard the way most families stared at TV. Sal was sharing beef jerky from a gristle-thick plastic bag of Jumbo Fiery Hot Strips, and they were drinking from plastic liter bottles of water filled that afternoon from a neighbor's poorly-guarded backyard spigot.

"What I was like, how I acted, the places I've been. I don't know why they'll want to know; it's just the way people are. They need to establish interest in people outside themselves, or else they find it difficult getting out of bed. If you play your cards right, and remember everything I tell you, then you'll be the only person in the world who can help them understand me, and how far I went, and everything I learned along the way. Like there was this one house, I don't remember where exactly, or who lived in it, or what they fixed me for breakfast. But in the basement they had this huge cardboard box, bigger than you and me put together. And when nobody was looking, I could crawl into this box and close the flaps behind me, and smell the completeness of myself, and forget everything, it was like nothing else mattered. I was just Sal in the box and nobody else. And if you can remember that story, and can tell it to the people who ask about me, then you'll be the only person in the entire world who knows that one moment of my existence as perfectly as I do. You can keep me alive even after I'm dead, which is especially comforting to me lately. Because if things turn out how I expect, when my travels are concluded, I'll probably have a very short and uneventful life. It's not something I wish for, by the way. But when you get to my age, you can start reading every bend in the road."

The trick about writing books, Sal soon realized, is that you could only perform the secret of yourself when nobody was listening. And that was easier said than done.

"Little girls? Hello? I know you're in there. Would you please let me in? My name is Mr Stillworth, and I work for the State Board of Child Rescue Services. I just need to speak with either you or your daddy for a few moments. I promise not to outstay my welcome. I just need to assure myself that you aren't in urgent need of attention, and that your basic requirements are being met. We don't seem to have any records of two little girls registered at this address, and we're curious about where you came from, and whether this is your legal residence or not. Have you registered with a doctor or health care provider in the area? Have you registered with the schools – it doesn't appear so, not from my records anyway. Childhood is a precious national resource, little girls. It should never be wasted or taken for granted. It needs to be cherished and cultivated. And, whenever possible, it needs to be made one with God, or any credible Higher Power, or whatever binding universal force is most agreeable to your native background and individual personality profile. Do you understand where I'm coming from, little girls? I'm coming from an organization that knows everything there is to know about little girls except the bare facts. Facts such as your names, your birthplaces, and, if you have them, your social security numbers."

Mr Stillworth never actually arrived at their door; it was more as if he precipitated from the atmosphere, like karma or bad weather. Some days he would stand on the patio and simply lean his weight against the door, not saying a word, picking at hangnails or aimlessly tapping at the brass-lidded mail slot with a thick blue ball-point pen. He whistled little tunes that Sal half recognized, tunes rich with cheerful opinions about love, and God, and the all-embracing nature of humanity. Mr Stillworth was willing to share these positive, uplifting opinions even when Sal and the little sister showed no interest in opening the door to let him in.

"*Lah dee dum, little girls, little girls,*" Mr Stillworth sang, his shoulder heavy against the slender door frame. "*Always love, always hope, little girls, little girls.*" Parts of the tune were a bit like "Camptown Races," and other parts were a bit like "Silent Night." Mr Stillworth could sing like this for hours until his thin, clattery voice infiltrated everything, like the high humming power lines, or the ambient rush of cars on the freeway. He was so much there it was like he wasn't there at all. And once you heard his voice for the first time, it was hard to imagine the universe without him.

"It's not me they're interested in," Daddy explained, the last time Sal ever saw him as an independent person who loved her. "They're only interested in you. They want to take you back to the time before I found you and turn you into one of them. We're talking about the bus to Normal Town, Sal, a small sub-urb on the outskirts of a large city, with carefully diagrammed public spaces, and lots of really interesting educational activities for kids of every age and religious background. Weirdly culti-vated little parks and playgrounds, bicycle racks and concrete water fountains and flaking metal jungle gyms. Then there's this dog-run composed of dry brown dirt where your animals are supposed to relieve themselves on command, and you're sup-posed to clean up after them with a pair of clear plastic gloves, as if even nature should be ashamed of its most basic creaturely urges. There's a yellow police call box which hasn't worked in years, and something called a Community Center, an alumi-num-sided quadrangular building with padded floors in which men and women with bad haircuts perform yoga, aerobics, and community service, or discuss their years of victimization while enjoying the mutual support of other victims just like them. The weirdest part about this place, Sal, is that you keep seeing the same faces over and over again, but none of them makes an impression. You see them again and again but you can't ever remember who they are, or why they need you so much. You keep thinking you *should* recognize them but you don't. Young people, old people, really old people, completely interchange-able sad people, people without a single interesting thing to talk about all day except you. Even your own parents, Sal – they aren't any different from everybody else. Just a couple of dull, well-meaning kids with office jobs who don't know how to activate a stupid pilot light on their stupid boiler without hiring some idiot like myself to do it for them. I've been living off people like your parents all my life, Sal. They couldn't light a match without an instruction booklet, and a one-nine-hundred number for contacting other stupid people to support them in their hour of need. That's what they want to take you back to, Sal. A place so meaningless that somebody as meaningless as me could take you from it. I just hope you'll consider all the options before you make your decision, kid. Not that there are many options. But I think you know what I mean."

———

On the night he went away, Daddy waited until the little sister was asleep, and Sal helped him carry cardboard boxes out to the van. Most of the boxes were filled with old newspapers and magazines, random slats of nail-studded lumber, dirt-stained work gloves, and a peculiar assortment of dirty bolts, screws, and miniature knickknacks that might have been looted from some third-rate carpenter's basement.

"I know I haven't been the greatest father in the world," Daddy confided to Sal as they arranged the loosely rattling cardboard boxes in back of the van. "I keep a safe distance from most people, and I'm not very affectionate. But at least I never tried to pervert your natural desires for affection – I just steered clear of them. At the same time, it gets awfully boring after a while, trying to understand little girls, and I'm afraid I'm not up to the task. I need something more meaningful from life, a sense of distance and perspective. A room where I can close the door behind me, and a regular income where I don't have to work so much, like maybe an academic career in the social sciences, or something in government. Like being a foster father, for example. I'd be pretty good at that. These various children could come to my house and live with me, and I could teach them the ropes of living an alternative lifestyle and so forth. Then, once they knew how to play the game, they'd be adopted by sensible couples with stable lifestyle arrangements, and go away again. Then other kids would come stay with me, learn the ropes, and move on, sort of like an assembly line. Everything would be clearly defined from the start. There'd be no getting tangled up in pointless emotional commitments, or false expectations. It's like we'd be saying goodbye already before we even met."

You don't change in your relationship to other people, Sal thought, watching Daddy nestle into his beaded driver's seat, toss the frayed gray ribbons of the seat-belt out of his way, and gaze out the wide smudgy window at empty streets. You change in your relationship to yourself. It's just that sometimes other people see it happening and try to get involved in the process.

"If we need you," Sal said, "how do we reach you?" It would be one of the only questions Sal ever asked Daddy, since theirs had never been a question-answer sort of relationship. It had always been more of a live-and-let-live sort of deal.

"I don't know, honey. Maybe look me up in the phone book? You know how to work a phone book, don't you, Sal?"

Sal thought about this for a moment. Then said:

"It's a book of numbers, names, and addresses. It tells you how to contact all the people you don't want to know."

Daddy didn't always listen when Sal said things. It was one of his charms.

"That's right, honey. Numbers and the names of people you'll never meet. And that goddamn phone company practically gives them away."

For the next few days or so, Sal didn't tell the little sister anything about what had happened. She simply performed old routines, and manufactured enough words to sustain them.

"Okay, we'll play the tea-time deal for another hour or so, or just long enough that I don't actually go completely crazy from the mindless repetition. Then we'll take a walk, and do some shopping. We're completely broke until, you know, Daddy gets back, so we'll have to do the teamwork thing at the market again. You drift off down one of the aisles and start crying or spill something, and while you're raising hell, I'll stuff my pockets full of canned beans and hash. By the time they've fed you a couple lollipops, I'll show up and play the bashful-but-capable-little-girl number. They can't seem to get enough of that one. Mostly, though, I want us to get back to the book we're writing, and discuss some people I've left out. For example, I've completely forgotten to mention the people at social services, and the Deputy District Attorney, and some almost-completely-forgettable support-staff. And don't worry if you can't remember every detail. Just listen, absorb, and let the stuff seep in. You need to *become* the book, not remember it. Otherwise, it'll be like none of these people ever mattered."

The little sister rarely said anything after Daddy left; she just served pretend-tea, or presented Sal with pretend-cake, and whenever she was reduced to eating real food she chewed it with a placid, local intensity. She wasn't much, Sal thought, but she was dependable. And dependable was all Sal needed right now.

"People are always trying to get you to do things, or go places," Sal told her, even at night while the little sister was sleeping. She would hold the little girl's pale, mud-stained hand and read the pulse of her blood as if it were a pattern of tea leaves at the bottom of a cup. "They're like these forces of nature, all rattling around in the same basement, trying to find a way out. But there isn't any way out, so they keep banging against each other, repeating themselves in each other's ears until they can't hear anything but themselves. Surprise, happiness, fear, anxiety, loneliness, sadness, loss. There simply aren't that many things to experience when you live in a basement. You have to keep covering the same ground, constantly pretending that everything that happens is totally unexpected and new."

Sal began to dream for the first time in her life, as if someone had thrown a switch in her head, activating a sub-system of sensation that was almost as strange, beautiful, and predictable as real life. Often she dreamed of the flooded basement, with spiny crocodiles gliding underneath the green water, or Daddy swinging the oars of a rowboat like the clumsy wings of some huge mechanical bird. But just as often, she dreamed of Mr Stillworth, who sometimes unzipped himself from Daddy's skin as if he were removing a long winter overcoat. Suddenly, they weren't in the basement anymore. They were standing in a wide concrete underground parking lot flanked by endless rows of station wagons and SUVs.

"This isn't a world for little girls and boys without mommies and daddies to protect them," Mr Stillworth told her, approaching her dream-self as if she were a wild dog, extending the back of one limp hand so she could sniff him. "This is a world where innocence is preyed upon by vast supernatural forces. Sometimes these forces disguise themselves as school teachers, hospital orderlies, and friendly old ladies who greet you in high-class hotel restrooms. They offer you candy, and compliments, and promise to introduce you to their pets. Then they lure you into their cars by promising to play your favorite songs on the cd player, or by buying you fast food with ketchup. They drive you to remote locations where you don't recognize the landmarks; they ask you to trust them. Eventually, they pull over and stop the car and tell you what *they* want. Until now, it's all been about you. What-you-want, what-makes-you-happy. But suddenly it's all about *them*. It's like you don't even exist."

Some mornings, Sal awoke where she had fallen asleep in the front hallway to find that Mr Stillworth's voice wasn't a dream. He was standing outside their front door, breathing an odor of ham and eggs through the mail slot, emitting little snip, snip sounds as if he were either snapping gum with his teeth or trimming his fingernails.

"Are you ready to come with me?" he asked. "I've spoken with Mrs Mayhew and she says you like vanilla ice cream. Your name's Stephanie, or at least that's what you told her. I think I know where we can find us some vanilla ice cream, Stephanie. Then, maybe you'll tell me your real name. Would you do that for me, Stephanie? That would sure put us one up on old Mrs Mayhew, wouldn't it? That would definitely teach Mrs Mayhew a thing or two."

The little sister liked to insert objects in her mouth and test them with her tongue, or draw their tips across her stippled palette with a convoluted and inward expression, as if she were imagining the surface of an alien planet. She didn't care what it was, either; if it fit her mouth, her mouth took it. Pieces of stray wood or plastic, matchbook covers and bottle caps, broken pencils or crayons. She put everything she found to this intimate modular use, as if she were continually reassessing the world by means of some invisible oral geometry.

"Put that away," Sal told her. "Don't suck on that. Where did you find that anyway? You don't even know where that's been."

But the little girl never removed these objects from her mouth, even when she was told to. She simply rolled her eyes towards Sal in an expression of roving, uncommitted curiosity. This tastes like this, her eyes said. And Sal says things like that. It was as if her manifold senses and experiences had been reduced to one simple impression. How things tasted. Or how other people thought they did.

"You're making me sick to my stomach," Sal said. They were sitting on a high sloping green lawn overlooking the Buzzy Bee Day-Care Center. A pale colorless light was assembling in the slopes and eddies of the grassy hillside. "Please take that out of your mouth. Please listen to what I'm trying to say. What you see down below is one of those institutions Daddy took us from. If you're not careful, it's the exact same type of institution that will take us back and never let us go. Banks, mortgage lenders, grammar schools, retirement funds, estate fees, tax people, and hospitals filled with doctors and nurses who don't even like the look of one another, let alone a bunch of sick losers like us. Every one of these institutions has a set of forms to sign, rules to obey, rooms to sleep in. If they had their way, we'd never be allowed to leave. The only thing we'd be permitted to know would be *them*. *Their* houses, and *their* rules. Now look, how are you going to learn anything if you don't listen to me? Please take that out of your mouth. Is it some sort of electrical cord? Is that dog poop on the end? Where do you find these things anyway? I didn't even see you pick it up. It's dirty and it smells."

The way she sucked, it might have been an ice cream cone, or a stick of hard candy, or a peach pit juicy with pulp. It was non-negotiable and inviolable and hers.

This is all I need, the little girl said with her eyes. This thing in my mouth and you.

HAD TO BE GONE

It was as if the world had taken everything Sal loved and ruined it, turned it against her somehow, and returned it in such miserable condition that she didn't even want it anymore. You just can't keep young in a world like this one, Sal thought. Eventually, it corrupts everybody and makes them all the same.

"This is how you lift the latch," Sal explained to her little sister on the last morning they spent together before Mr Stillworth arrived in his chromium blue SUV to perform his morning vigil on the porch. "I'll put the orange crate here so you can reach, but be careful. A couple of these slats are loose; these nails are coming out, and you might cut yourself. Now, I've left some whole grain cereal in the kitchen, and several bottles of fairly clean water from the backyard tap on the windowsill. Remember, only leave when you're *ready* to leave, not when they *tell* you to. If you feel any hesitation, go downstairs, sit in the basement, and lock all the doors. When Mr Stillworth punches off around five thirty, you can slip out the back. Travel mainly at night, but wash your face and comb your hair first; you'll get better mileage that way. Nobody wants to pick up a dirty little girl with dirty shoes. Especially when they've just cleaned the car."

The little girl was leaning against the door and sucking on something that resembled a rusty metal lozenge. It left speckled red dots on the corners of her mouth.

"On the other hand," Sal said, "if you decide to go with Mr Stillworth, then nobody will hold it against you, certainly not me. He can give you all the things Daddy and I never could. But whatever you decide, and however things turn out, be kind to yourself afterwards. Nothing ever works out perfect in this life. We just do the best we can and move on."

———————

The skies were blue and clear on the morning Sal resumed her former life, traversing the roads and vistas of the forgotten world with a faded gray cloth knapsack hitched over one shoulder, and a sense of restless yearning in her heart. She found the knapsack hidden away in the ruined backyard, a wet whorl of gray bulk-cotton that had lain like a huge thumbprint amidst the matted gray weeds and mud, as if flung there from the belly of a passing aircraft. The cloth was so soft and worn that it possessed the texture of gray felt, and after she washed it under the dripping tap and dried it in the misty sun, it was large enough to hold two loaves of bread, a liter of water, and a tin of Pringles Sour-Cream and Chives potato chips. Sal didn't like Pringles, but she appreciated anything with a pop-top tab, especially one that released a tiny explosion of compressed air when you pulled the tin lid from its hard tubular category of air. Most of all, she liked the fact that you didn't need a can opener to open it.

She didn't see another human being for the next several days or weeks; time seemed to have run out on her; she wasn't even sure how the world could fall behind so quickly, or what sort of boundary she had crossed to reach this place she had never imagined before. Great orangish rocks and mountains lifted up around her, eruptions of formlessness and craggy declaration that had nothing to tell her about who she was or where she had been. From a distance, everything looked unattainable and impossible – the broken black jagged rifts of crusty ground, the twisted peaks of anthill-like rocks and precipices, and the gray-white foam of clouds that covered the sky like a break in service on some television program that nobody ever watched. It was funny, Sal thought, how quickly you forgot people when they weren't around. Even the people you were leaving.

And then, at some point in her outward journey, weather found Sal, as if it had been looking for her all along. One evening, while she slept under a fallen pasteboard sign without any readable words on it, heavy rains broached the sky and didn't let up for three days, drenching Sal in an excess of atmosphere that streamed off her skin and clothes in little mockeries of rivers and soft avalanches. No matter how fast she walked, the winds blew water off her skin and face in spinning translucent sheets, flaunting them like the sails of some ghost ship. It was as if weather was both riding and encompassing Sal, driving her into the same forces she resisted – rushing gales, brief rattling blizzards of hail, and abrupt conic vortices of dust that arose from the sands around her like spectral guardians, shiftily dodging her glances when she looked at them and dogging her steps when she didn't. She couldn't even see other animals out here, that was the part that worried her. Thousands of holes punctuated the ground in every direction, as if this sheet of planet had been struck by tiny meteors from a moon-sized air-gun. No gophers or rabbits popped their heads out of these holes. They were homes only to themselves.

I've been sent here to understand, Sal realized one morning, when the lightening-showers intensified to a point where even the ground thundered. It was the first time she had ever been awoken by color – a horizon of roiling clouds and blinding refractions that burst from the unseen world she was staggering toward. I'm not looking for the things I usually look for, or even for those intermittent people who once helped me find my way. I don't need a place to sleep, or somebody to feed me, or even directions to the next public restroom. It was as if the world's limiting mechanisms had stopped operating long enough for Sal to find a way out of it. She didn't need people and houses anymore. All she needed was volition.

For the first several days, Sal lacked neither nourishment nor moisture. She drank straight from the sky, and filled her plastic Evian bottle with curtains of rain billowing past. She fed on wild raspberries and tiny hard-bitten crabapples that lay strewn across the thorny, thistly carpets of scraggly oases. Then, as the landscape changed, it brought new types of weather – heat from the sun, dry motions of air moving past, and visionary pulses that rose off the hard ground in waves of non-meaning that drew Sal further into the heat. Coyotes grew prevalent; soil grew sandier. Eventually, the rains ceased, and as the water evaporated from Sal's corrugated plastic bottle, her insides turned parched and bristly. If she had any voice left, her throat wouldn't release it. When she stroked her thin arms, her skin lacked resiliency; she could push the integument loosely back and forth, like a cheap toupe on the head of a bald man.

I used to be small, but now I'm not small anymore, Sal thought as she walked into the always-increasing distance. Her legs didn't function as well as they once did; she staggered over little boulders of heat that clambered up from the desert floor like spiders. I used to be the one that people held in their arms. But until I found weather, I never understood how big things really are. I encompass my own vistas, breathe my own air, ponder my own worlds. And if I stand firm, nobody can make me do otherwise. I can imagine my own types of weather.

———

That night, Sal suffered terrible visions of catastrophe and annihilation. Earthquakes struck the hard earth like fists, and huge crevasses opened down the sides of black mountains, spewing flames and red lava. In faraway cities, the people who once loved Sal were visited by calamities they didn't deserve: mobs tore them apart with large metal wrenches and gardening implements; hurricanes crashed through their homes and garages; and shattered glass rained down on everybody left standing like an afterthought. Everything Sal knew about the world seemed to be diminishing.

When Sal woke, she lay frying in the white sun. The shadows of trees avoided her, and, only a few yards away, coyotes muttered together like conspirators, eyeing her depleted gray knapsack which lay on the ground like an expired balloon. When she returned their gazes, they padded away. They didn't want to test her. They just wanted to know where she was.

The entire world that Sal loved was suddenly far behind her, and as she staggered across the white plain, she decided not to look back. Don't love things that don't last, Sal thought. Just take what you need. Move on. Keep it new. Life is all that matters until it's over. And once it's over, never go back.

She walked until her pink shoes fell off and her white socks wore through. She sipped moisture from the limbs of cacti that she broke open like weird cucumbers, and turbaned her hair with strips of pink cloth torn from the hem of her unraveling pink dress. She fed on speckled gray eggs from twiggy nests, small leathery lizards that weren't quick enough, and the burred polyps of wildflowers, sucking anything soft and perishable into her mouth and making it hers. As she journeyed further towards the sun that was destroying her, rabbits burst from the gray brush in succinct little explosions. Prairie dogs and gophers arose from holes in the ground, their withered paws poised, as if practicing subservience. But you don't owe anybody anything, Sal thought. Nobody is better than you. We're all the same: hungry and thirsty and mired in bad weather.

Her body and mind grew harder, more compact and attentive; she wasn't the same old boring no-nothing Sal anymore. *I'm not trying to go anywhere, or leave anything behind*, she reminded herself.

She had collapsed in some sort of sticky yellow sand, legless and palpitating; her eyes flickered; she couldn't focus on anything long enough to see it. *I'm heading nowhere at my own pace. I don't even care if I get there. It's just the me and the not-me. It's the thing about picking yourself up and trying again. That stuff people are always telling you – whether you're listening or not.*

Sometimes she lay on the hot dirt for hours, shielding her eyes from the sun with the inverted V of her elbow, splayed across herself like a broken doll. She tasted the dryness of her own mouth; she figured the shape of old substances with her tongue. Then, when she couldn't even visualize getting to her feet and walking, she submitted to the hard ground and tried to remember the faces of the people who had watched her pass by. They kept staring without paying attention, their faces filled with too much information. They were all different but she couldn't tell them apart. They're so hard to write down, Sal thought. Why is everybody self-conscious? None of this matters. And it makes them so hard to remember.

When the sun set and the cold black night stepped forth from itself, Sal managed movement again. She kicked at the ground with her feet, propelling herself sideways in little jolts, like the snake she had severed one morning with a sharp rock. Eventually, these intermittent pulses of intention landed her on a knee or an elbow; she found traction; her body either yielded to gravity or gravity yielded to her, and every time she stood, it felt like for the first time; she had to learn balance again. The stars were massed against her, splashing the night with radiance, one tiny blazing world after another. Go back, they said. Turn around. You can never be so beautiful as us. You can never be so bright.

It was as if they angered her blood, these oceans of stars beating against the beach of her. And as she moved forward, limping in a hundred different directions at once, she learned to trust the simple integrity of herself. It was just a matter of taking steps and fulfilling them. It was little more than an exercise of judgment.

Some books can't be finished, Sal thought. And some people can't be written down.

It made her angry and vain.

You're not being fair, she thought back at the stars, as if she were returning a wicked volley on the tennis court of her imagination. You can't tell me what to do. You can't not love me, or not know me. Get used to it. I'm already here.

———

She began measuring time as a series of endurances. There was the endurance of pain, the endurance of bad feet, the endurance of stars, the endurance of laughter, and the endurance of weird trees. But sometime after the endurance of altered perspective, Sal entered a period that wasn't so easily quantifiable. Later, she called it the endurance of animals. But as it was happening, it seemed more like the endurance of self-awareness, or conversion, or heat.

She had been walking up a steep slope, her relationship with gravity under continual reassessment. She couldn't tell if she was leaning forward or backward, and something hissed behind her ears, as if she were releasing steam. The colors of the sky resembled the muted pastels of a comic book, with pixilated air like sand, and clouds like empty dialog bubbles. At intervals, animals appeared and vanished again, poking up from the ground, or perching on trees and rocks, like targets in a shooting gallery. A military formation of high power lines appeared in the distance, and Sal didn't know whether she should continue heading towards them, or just turn around and leave them behind. Perhaps they were a warning. This is your last chance, they were saying. Now please go away.

"From now on," a voice said from the desert, "you will be sufficient unto yourself. You will endure everything but salvation. You will pitch your tent in the night, and find food in strange places. Under rocks, and in the shadows of trees. You will hide in the earth, clinging to texture; even wolves will protect you. Exhausted by the company of people, you will enjoy the simple expressions of animals, who can't bother you with stupid words, or sentences, or their barely-considered dreams of coherence and meaning."

It was a scrawny orange coyote with a skinless gray patch of loose skin slung over one shoulder. Sal didn't know how long the coyote had been following her, but it seemed to anticipate her progress, drifting just ahead and to the right of her like a kite. You meet a lot of unusual creatures in this world, Sal thought. You can't be expected to remember each of them by name.

"You'll need to maintain integrity and distance when you go back," the coyote said. "Or develop hobbies that force you to spend time with material things. Stamps, bottle caps, coins, native American jewelry, whatever. When you're older, it might be model trains or dolls, the classic collectible kind with parchment-yellow skin and crumbling taffeta dresses. The point isn't what you think so much as what you *don't*. You don't need to think about the world, for example. Or weather, or people. Those things just got you into trouble. They drew you away from the deeper reality of yourself."

It was funny how a coyote could walk and talk at the same time, its body cruising at an angle, like a sailboat tacking into a wind-roused harbor. He was always getting closer and always moving further away. Sal wondered if there was a word to express a contradiction like that. Synergy was a term she had heard. Dynamics. Orbital velocity. Divinity. Hope.

For the first time in ages, Sal recalled the sunflower in Mrs Anderson's garden, hunched in cynical observation of the world around it. She recalled the Unhappy Man, and the anonymous succession of Laundromats, and the vending machines that had assumed different personalities in her life, from dour and unresponsive to prosperous and sad. She recalled the unseen rooms of Social Services, where other children sat silent and alone in their proportionate spaces, trying to hear themselves think. Then there was Mrs Mayhew's car, and the way Daddy hadn't looked back when he drove away, and the small huddled darknesses nestled in a pool of damp blankets that might have been somebody like herself, she wasn't entirely sure. A distant and hypothetical quality of attention, like a Martian with a telescope. Tethered to its awareness of things and people. Unable to retreat from or move any closer to the world it was observing. Just like Sal.

Nobody knew she was coming. She hadn't sent ahead any cards or letters, or performed smoke signals with a campfire and a flapping burlap blanket. She simply reached the end of her isolation and said goodbye. It never felt like arriving. It always felt like going away.

"If you need us, you know where to find us," the coyote said. They had achieved the summit of a brown flinty hill. When Sal kicked a flat stone down the slope, it carried other rocks with it, and those rocks carried other rocks, with a clattery chime-like momentum. "You can find us at the pet shop or the zoo. We're in the sky; we're in the bushes; we're in the oceans; we're in the trees. If things work out, we won't bother you anymore. We'll let you learn things for yourself."

The house resembled a mockery of houses, as if its knotty planks and twisted iron nails were rejects from all the decent ones in decent neighborhoods. The windows didn't even have glass in them, just sheets of muslin thumb-tacked to the frames like rabbit pelts. A phalanx of green twiggy branches lay heaped under a half-framed plastic tarp, and an old, well-rounded car without any wheels kneeled like an ancient, bone-weary dog trying to beg. The man on the front porch, bearded and long-haired, seemed both really old and really young at the same time, drinking amber liquid from a long-stemmed wine glass. He didn't get up or offer to help. He just watched her lean over a dented aluminum bucket and pour water into her mouth with a rusty metal ladle.

This might be okay, Sal thought, tasting the water. I could sleep in a house like this. I could drink water that tastes like this. I could let a man like that watch me do things. I could even help with the chores.

The old young man wasn't in any hurry to do anything. His chapped lips took the remaining amber liquid from the tall-stemmed wine glass. Then he replaced the empty glass on an almost-porous-looking checkerboard side-table. It was clear to Sal that this amber liquid pleased the old young man very much.

He licked his chapped lips like a lizard on a rock.

"Do you know what it means," he asked Sal, "when a half-naked little girl emerges from the desert in the remains of a pink cotton dress?"

Sal felt tiny pops and bubbles of sound emerge from her throat. She didn't have to answer if she didn't want to. She never had to play second-banana to anybody ever again.

The old young man showed her perfect white teeth in a face that was neither white nor perfect.

"It means," the old young man said, "that this stupid old world has one more chance."

She refused to sleep or dream or lose one moment of that perfect awareness she had traveled so far to find. Instead, she lay awake in her own subsidence, like a leaf after a storm, watching the sun rise and set through leaking muslin curtains, stretching her mouth forward to take water from the now-familiar ladle being delivered periodically by the old young man, just as she had seen flowers reach for the minute presentations of a honeybee, or a dog sniff a bone. Life is a sequence of omissions, she thought. You never get that little bit extra you're waiting for. You can't live your life expecting to suck up every last little drop.

If Sal had died, her world might look like this. A broken house, a slanting cot, mounting increments of water. In one corner of the room stood a huge crooked medley of empty birdcages, metal mouths hanging open, scored wooden perches rimed with nitrates. In another corner, a set of *Reader's Digest Condensed Books* were stacked like totems, their chipped cloth bindings designed to resemble hand-cured leather. Extinguished white candles were mounted on cracked white plates, or protruded from the mouths of wax-skirted wine bottles. The old young man had been here so long he had granted a sense of entitlement even to rubbish. Everything belonged here, even Sal.

"When we die," the old young man said, sitting on the edge of Sal's cot and stroking her forehead with a cool, wet rag, "we go somewhere that looks like this. All the things we ever loved become furniture. The hollowness we feel turns into a house. There aren't any other people in it, and that's one of its blessings. It's just filled with the ghosts of objects we used to own, things we used to feel, memories of patience and heat. And the best part of it, little girl, is that we can finally stop looking forward to meaningless events, like who we'll meet next, or what will happen when they leave. In the after-life, everything is already over. We don't have anything to regret, or anything to look forward to. We can lie back and drink water from a rusty ladle. We can appreciate the birdcages that once belonged to dead birds."

Sal adjusted to a more formal sequence of nights and mornings, lying on the cot and sipping green water, examining the discord of bird cages as if she were remembering a former life. Once, long ago, she had flitted from one perch to another. She had sipped water from plastic bowls and shelled seeds from plastic cups. Whenever she took flight, she encountered limits to what she was. It couldn't even be considered flying. It felt more like a series of aeronautically-propelled little twitches.

"You never escape anything," the old young man told her. "Especially not children. You think you can escape them, and you imagine all sorts of exciting places you might go to get away from them, but they always find you, even when the tax people can't. They pester you for nickels and affection. They show you all the dirty things they found in the street, and introduce you to their dollies, and ask endless questions about nothing, not because they want to hear your answers, but because they appreciate the routine effort of one person talking and another person not listening. The worst thing about children is that they're everywhere, like they've got your number already, you can't fool them for a second. Every country you visit, every city, every street, breaking your neck with their mislaid skates and Hot Wheels, their plastic robots and smelly, water-stained coloring books. That's the thing about children that always finds you, little girl: the smell you can't get rid of, not even with white vinegar. And the smell of all those dead, meaningless things they leave behind."

———

It's better when the world comes looking for you, Sal thought, lying on the rocky mattress with the damp white dishcloth on her forehead, feeling it turn dry and crispy at the edges before the old young man came to rinse it in a bucket and apply it to her forehead again. When you go into the world, you waste energy and momentum. You find yourself stranded in strange places. Dogs bark; you sleep in parking lots; and people pretend not to look at you, even when you're right under their noses. It's never you that matters. It's only where you've been, and who you know.

"We just need to see her for a moment," one woman said. "Ask her if she remembers Aunt Sophie and Uncle Tod, and show her this ceramic pig. Here, I'll unwrap the tissue and you go inside and show it to her, we haven't got all day. If she doesn't remember either Aunt Sophie or this ceramic pig, we promise to go away and never come back. We'll figure she's not the same girl we're looking for and call off the lawyers. We don't want to cause problems. We just want to give her a chance to remember where she came from. And the sort of people who helped her along the way."

But the old young man held the door partly closed. He didn't need any weight in his body, or authority in his voice, to hold his position. "She's asleep," he told them. "And she doesn't remember any Aunt Sophie. Now please get off my property. I don't want to sound corny or threatening, but this is my property and you better leave."

"It's not just Aunt Sophie," the woman said louder, as if she were sending her voice ahead to check out the territory. "It's Aunt Sophie and Uncle *Tod*! Ask her if she remembers leaving notes out for the milkman! Or that time we lost our car at the airport! Ask her just one of these simple questions and we promise to leave!"

In her bed, Sal couldn't see out the window; she couldn't even reach far enough to test the hem of the frail, unraveling curtain. She could only detect vague shapes beyond her window, clouds and plants and mountains, and the even vaguer shadows of cars as they came grinding up the rocky driveway with the dry intimate sound of concrete in a mixer.

"She's asleep," the old young man said. "She doesn't know you, and she doesn't want to know you. Now turn your car around and head back to the main road. Make a right, drive ten miles, and you'll see a sign for the onramp. Get on that goddamn onramp and go away."

It wasn't like time anymore; it didn't feel like clocking up miles on an odometer, or making progress across space. It was more like primitive accumulation, the gathering of raw matter: gold, dirt, buttons, wax. The old young man never asked her any questions, or expected her to ask him any questions in return. He fed her beef broth, soft unpeeled yellow carrots from the weedy garden, and barely warmed-up cans of Hormel's Chili Con Carne with beans. He neither boiled nor chilled the rusty water he brought to her in a ladle each morning and night, as if it were a consecration, some peculiar and overdressed ritual Sal had witnessed in a church long ago. Occasionally, he took one of the empty bird cages with him when he left and hurled it clattering into a large woodpile beyond the garden, where it erupted in a chirruping of flightless birds and weirdly rattling creatures who came scurrying outwards from the impact like the emanations of a stone in a pond. Sometimes the creatures scurried through the cabin, rattling under the floorboards or bouncing from wall to wall like small furry rubberized projectiles.

The cabin never felt more porous or insubstantial than when these animals disappeared into it.

"Did a green scaly thing come darting through here?" the old young man said. He was wearing cutoff gray sweatpants and a pair of mismatched gardening gloves. The hair on his chest was gray and matted like stained leather. "I couldn't tell if it was a lizard or a snake. Thought maybe I'd fry it in a little corn oil or maybe some cocoa butter. A lot of people don't appreciate the ability of cocoa butter to make a meal out of strange food, but then people don't know lots of things. For instance, these so-called friends of yours who keep visiting, they don't even know your name, or where you're from. They just seem to've heard about this little girl who emerged from the desert with muscles in the backs of her legs like strips of copper cable, and this far off look about her. And well behaved? You've never seen anything like it – *hey*! What was that? Did that look green to you? Mean little bastard. One of these days I'm going to burn this place to the ground and there won't be anywhere left for them to hide. And anytime I feel like it, I'll scoop them out of the sand with a shovel and bite off their goddamn heads."

Sometimes the people arrived in groups and filed into the front room with low voices and careful footsteps, like tardy mourners proceeding through a cramped mausoleum. They acted both bashful and arrogant, whispering unfamiliar thoughts, as if every object evoked some secret indication of Sal.

"She probably sits on that chair," they said. "She probably drinks water out of that cup, and watches the sky through that window, and spends her time absorbed by moral complexities that we can't even imagine, because we're so far beneath her plane of awareness it's ridiculous. She only looks like a little girl on the surface, but underneath she's a major intellectual. She's come to teach us how to be better, and kinder, and wiser than we usually are. Like that water glass – just look. Those are probably *her* fingerprints – don't *touch* it, Sammy! I said look at it, don't touch! That's not some play toy. That's an object of veneration. Here, let me get a picture. Take a picture of me standing right here and I'll point at it, see? Here's me pointing at the glass with *her* fingerprints on it. Just wait for the green light to come on, and push that gray button on the side."

The problem with people, Sal thought in her bed in back of the cabin, is that they only come around when you don't want them. And of course whenever you need one, they're nowhere to be found.

"Can we take her home?" a little girl was saying in the driveway. When people spoke outside, their voices seemed to be transmitted through every board of the house, as if it were a sort of sonic honeycomb. "She's probably really bored, and would enjoy a drive in our car. Why don't we take her back to our house and let her watch me play with my toys. I'm sure she's never seen a house as nice as ours. I'm sure she's never seen so many nice toys."

The old young man continued bringing her the rusty ladle filled with water. He cooked her canned broth on the stove, guarded the bedroom doorway with his unsubstantiated threats of gun-ownership, and always reported straight back to Sal as soon as the visitors drove their dusty cars back up the unglimpsable gravel road to the even more-unglimpsable main road into town. He was the most proficient and dependable adult Sal had ever known.

"They left you these photos in an album," the old young man said, tossing the latest offerings onto the clattery disassembly of bird cages, where they accumulated day after day like sacrificial mementos in an end-of-civilization bonfire. "They left you these brand-new jumbo bags of little girl underpants and white socks. I told them not to come back, and not to tell their annoying friends and family about this place, but I don't think they heard me. In a few cases, I even offered them your autograph, which I scribbled on a paper towel in the pantry when they weren't looking. I'm starting to get the hang of these people, but I don't think I'll ever get the hang of where to put all this stupid stuff. Burnished coffee pots and frying pans. Tattered movie magazines and comic books with multi-racial super heroes. They say you used to live with them, or lived with somebody they knew, and they don't want you back or anything, they just want to make sure you're okay, and that you haven't forgotten them. And pictures – they're completely obsessed with taking pictures. Of me, the front door, the garden, the well. That's all the flashes you've been seeing, not thunder or weather or anything substantial. Just people with their Japanese cameras making personal history out of this house. Don't worry, little girl; I won't let them disturb you. But if they're real polite, I'll let them take pictures of your window. That way, they won't feel like they left something behind. Because when people feel like they left something behind, little girl, they always come back. Don't ask me why, neither. It's just the way people are."

The old young man was starting to smell of antiseptic hand soap, roll-on deodorant, and fluoridated toothpaste. One morning, after delivering Sal's rusty water, he sat on a pair of cubical, lead-colored bird cages and cut his hair with a pair of stainless steel scissors. He threw away his flip-flops and pulled on gray tennis shoes with broken yellow laces that looked like he dug them out of the yard. "You can't be caught standing around in your underpants when strangers come to visit," he explained through the scratchy snap, snap of the scissors. Even the roughness of his hands had turned smoother and less raspy, as if he had begun using a moisturizer. "You need to make a good first impression, or people won't take you seriously. They'll just think you're some stupid yoyo who lives in the desert and ignore everything you say. But the fact of the matter is that *I'm* the one you came to for sanctuary and comfort – not them. And it's high time they understood it. Or I might just stop talking to them altogether."

Later that day, the old young man washed the wooden floors with a green-handled broom, and wiped cobwebs from the ceiling with a dishrag tied to the end of a broken curtain rod. He clipped his fingernails with a pair of shearing scissors. He shaved.

———

"When can we see her?" the people asked, popping gaseous soda tabs on the patio, spraying their carbonated beverages everywhere like some spiritual disinfectant. "Are you sure you won't make an exception? We've come such a very long way."

The old young man wasn't quite so belligerent-sounding anymore.

"If I made an exception for you," he told them reasonably, "then I'd have to make an exception for everybody else."

"I heard she could predict Lotto and weather."

"I don't personally care about neither."

"Has she ever asked for anybody named Margie Delaware? She might not even know she was asking, or be halfway articulate about it. She might just mumble in her sleep, like 'Marzhy Delawhar,' but even more slurred. Kind of like I just said it right now. Only pretend I'm half asleep."

"She never says anything. But that's mainly because I don't ask her anything. It's not our sort of relationship. Me asking her things and then, you know. Her answering them."

"Ask if she's heard from my father. My father disappeared in the desert when I wasn't much older than she is now. But unlike her, my father never came back."

"I'm not asking her nothing for nobody."

"Hello! Little girl! Are you in there? Can you hear me? My name's Sadie, and I drove all the way from Detroit."

"Why don't you finish your orange soda in the car with your husband. If he keeps running that air conditioner, you're going to get yourself a dead battery before long."

"I need to learn about Margie Delaware! You don't have to be specific! You can speak in parables if you like! In fact, I'd kind of enjoy if you spoke in parables! It would make everything more interesting and profound, and make me feel more involved in the whole process of revelation. And my father – did you see my father out there? He went into the desert when I was a little girl and never came back!"

———————

The old young man began appearing in Sal's doorway holding a folded, pre-read newspaper, or a safety-corrugated paper cup of McDonald's coffee. He sewed denim patches over the holes in his shirt and pants, and began wearing what looked like somebody else's bifocals with chipped tortoiseshell frames. He put on weight, shaved on a semi-daily basis, and tried combing his hair in different directions. For a man of indeterminate age, he had a good head of hair on him. He just didn't have any idea what to do with it.

"I used to like it out here before we started getting so much company," he said. He wasn't actually talking to Sal; he was mainly talking to *them*. "I liked hearing the desert, and the leaning of the Joshua trees, and the deeper silence inside my own head. I'm not really into conversation or human society, which are both pretty over-rated, in my book. But at the same time, it's weird what happens when you start mixing with members of your own species again. It's like taking a shower, or buying a new pair of pants. You wake up refreshed every morning. You start feeling better about things. Like the way you look, or the person you used to be."

For the first few weeks, Sal felt at home in the old young man's bedroom. She took what was offered and never asked for anything else; she used the bedpan after dark, slipped it outside the open doorway when she was finished, and returned to the cot on her tiptoes, trying not to disturb the variously chittering animals that gathered under the floorboards when the old young man wasn't looking. When a board creaked, the hidden creatures skittered, or the old young man said something in the next room – muttering in his sleep or thinking out loud, it was all the same to Sal. Some creatures lived in the sunlight, and other creatures lived in the dark. It didn't make one creature better than any other creature. It was just the way their mommies and daddies had taught them to be.

"I'm sick of looking at this dump," the old young man explained one morning, about the same time a series of formidable-sounding vehicles began making progress down the graveled driveway. "All the things I should have done, or never finished doing, or thought about doing and decided screw it, who cares. Like these muslin curtains, for instance; they aren't any better than rags I found in the yard. Or these holes in the walls that should've been windows. I could install glass if I wanted; I'm perfectly capable. I've even got my old tools in the shed, probably some molding cement, if I looked hard enough. Or that goddamn wooden patio with all the nails sticking out of it; it's like a breeding ground for tetanus, I'm surprised nobody ever got hurt. Especially one of these, you know, these kids that come along with their parents. I'm warning you, little girl; you may see some serious changes taking place around this dump in the days ahead. Nobody's expecting you to help, understand. You just continue lying there if it makes you happy. But whatever you decide about staying or leaving, I'll still be here when you're gone. I might as well make myself comfortable in the meantime."

It began with the steady, persistent beat of a distant hammer, resounding through the sharp, dry air with a series of hard, immaculate cracks, like thick tree branches being snapped. Then it escalated into a medley of mutually-reassuring noises: the whirring of drills and lathes, the hish-hish of saws and adzes and sanding-planes and grooving files. Eventually, the tumbling of a concrete mixer infiltrated Sal's waking consciousness, and persisted until it became as pervasive as light, a continuous rolling bass accompaniment to everything the old young man did and said. The sound even encroached upon Sal's sense of herself, and the confluence of air and space and heat that divided her from the world and made her strong. She could hear the old young man breathing in hard, raspy breaths, as regular as the sound of his hammer, as he moved things around the yard, or in and out of the house, and Sal imagined herself sitting like the queen of an enormous chess board, surrounded by various knobby and angular pieces being moved in every direction, enforcing a structure both mathematical and progressive. Slatted wooden fences, bookcases, varnished mahogany table tops, henhouses, and storage sheds. It was growing less and less like isolation. It was turning into the sort of place that Sal had already been.

"Close your eyes," the old young man said on the day he tore the muslin curtains from the window. "Or cover your face with your arms. Your head won't like it at first. But that's the great thing about the head, little girl. It gets used to anything." Sal was already face down against the lumpy mattress, face coddled by the sticky sheets and feathery pillows, feeling her body sore and exposed in all the wrong places, like a tree uprooted from its foundations and left dying in the street. The curtains didn't make tearing sounds; they just fell away like shadows. After weeks of mismanagement and confusion, sunlight had found her. It would make her known all over again.

"Look at the world out there," the old young man said. He was striking the window-frame with a chisel. It sounded like someone scraping the barnacled underside of a boat. "It's got so much color in it, and so many interesting shapes and sounds. Just smell that sand and dirt, it's probably my favorite smell in the world. Moisten a handful with a little rainwater, hold it to your nose, and you'll know what I mean. Good enough to eat. And there, look. Mountains. Clouds. Trees. Plants. You can see the nearest city from here, where I'm pointing, see? It's something about these flat spaces and dry air. You can see the world coming from a hundred miles. Which gives you plenty of time to get the hell out of its way."

It wasn't even worth lying in bed anymore, Sal thought. The sun staring at her through the sparkling new glass window, faceted with refractions and adhesive-tape residue, and the bird-like manifestations of people outside in the yard holding up their children. "*See?*" they kept saying, as if it was the most important word they knew. "*See?* Didn't I tell you? Can you *see* her? *I* can see her – how about you?" It seemed to take all the integrity out of them, this act of seeing through windows. This leap they made through the window and back again.

While the old young man hammered in the yard, Sal sat on the sloping and irregularly shaped patio entertaining the families who brought offerings of canned goods, twenty dollar bills in white envelopes, and road maps with individual homes demarcated by stick-on glittery foil stars.

"Hi, my name is Sarah Fulton, and that's my husband out there in the car with our children, Susie and Roy. We're here to visit the little girl who emerged from the desert. Do you think she'll come out and say hello? I know she never makes exceptions, but maybe you could just ask. Tell her it's the Sarah

Fulton who works at the bank in Miguelito. Have you ever been to Miguelito, little girl? It's not worth the trip, believe me. But if you ever decide to visit Miguelito, come by the bank and ask for Sarah Fulton. Here's my card. It's got my phone number, but I'm easier to reach through e-mail. I hardly ever have time to answer the phone anymore."

Sal paid more attention to the reticent ones, like the muss-haired husband in the front seat of the dusty PT Cruiser playing a Nintendo DSi, or the two children in the back seat, leaning over his shoulder to watch.

"Come back later and I'll see what I can do," Sal told the woman after a while. She wondered why the women always came up so close, as if they were going to embrace her, even while they were craning their heads to see beyond her into the empty bedroom. "I think she's probably asleep now, or answering correspondence. She receives letters all the time from concerned people like yourself, but she doesn't have time to answer them all personally. Sometimes, she just sends a simple postcard, without any signature. She doesn't like to call attention to herself. She sort of expects you to know who it's from."

———————

For the next few days, Sal sat on the recently sanded patio in one of the new canvas deck chairs from Lands' End and watched the people come and go as the old young man hammered substance back into the shack, and formal clarity into all the shapes and structures surrounding it. And every time somebody went away, Sal imagined them following small roads that led into bigger ones. Eventually, there would be houses again, and thin saplings tied to wooden sticks, each one apportioned to an identically-sized rectangle of green grass. If Sal went with them, they might let Sal play with buttons on the dashboard, or activate the radio or cd player. They wouldn't tell her anything about themselves, but would encourage Sal to reveal lots of personal, deeply-felt things about herself.

"My name is Frank Morgan," said the man from California Social Services. "I don't normally deal with child-related welfare cases, but we've been really busy lately, so they asked me to lend a hand. Normally, I deal with probation issues concerning problem-teen offenders or, as I prefer to call them, repeat pre-adult criminal enactants. It's a pretty depressing line of work, and not my chosen path towards salvation at all. In fact, I've taken several extended leaves over the years, seeking a more productive development of my natural skills and resources, but they never pan out. I opened my own restaurant, tried on-line merchandising, customer relations, that sort of thing. I even tried teaching, but those kids, man. They really dragged me down. And every time I thought I'd found a way out of the probation service, I'd start drifting back in again, like my boat's caught in this wind-locked harbor and I can't get out. Now, I'm going to ask you a few questions, and then I'll go away. Then I'll come back in a few days with a court document, which I'll show to Mr Ludwig out there, the one planing that spruce door. Then I'll take you away and find you another place to live. It won't be the Four Seasons or anything, but it'll be better than a crooked bed in a desert shack without any doors. One step at a time, like they say in the program. Don't ask me which program, either. It's just one of those terms you pick up in my line of work."

Mr Morgan was the first man Sal had ever met who wore a tie every day and carried a beet-red leather briefcase. He drove a shapeless chromium gray vehicle that resembled the lidless gaze of a frog or a newt. His briefcase contained several sealed, brokenly-rattling plastic containers of Tic-Tacs, a porous flat gray recording device, and a phone directory. He would place the phone directory on whatever surface was available (in this case, the old young man's crooked and water-stained folding card-table) and place the recording device on the phone directory, as if he needed to cushion the world of words they were assembling, like a many-turreted castle glued together with popsicle sticks.

"This is Frank Morgan, acting representative for California State Child Welfare Service, case file seven seven six three four. Interview A for apple dash four four. Joshua Tree County, third of October. Commencing."

It was as if he were logging onto some interstellar spaceship.

"Would you please tell me your name?" He seemed to be interviewing the recording device, and expecting Sal to act as witness. "And where you're from?"

Sal heard the steady hish-hishing of the old young man outside planing wood. There was no stopping him, she thought. Pretty soon, he would be like everybody else.

"My name is Sal," she said. "And I've been on a journey."

"What sort of journey, Sal? Where has it taken you?"

Sometimes, Sal wasn't entirely certain when she was remembering things that had really happened, and when she was making them up. "Houses, mostly. Government buildings. And places like this. Places you only remember when you're actually in them."

She spread her arms, as if she were revealing her own sudden materialization in a field of flowers. Here I am, she thought. You thought I was over there, but I've been right here all along.

"Where do you come from originally?"

"From my mommy and daddy."

"And where do they live? And when was the last time you saw them?"

"A long time ago. When I was smaller."

"What do you remember about them? Do you remember their last names? Or any facial characteristics? What sort of car did they drive? What did they do for a living?"

There were no clouds outside. Sal liked when the sky got like that: the same all over.

"I don't remember anything important," she said finally. Frank Morgan was a very patient man; he deserved to learn something. "Except that my mommy mustn't have loved me enough to keep me. And my daddy drove a beautiful white van with these big cold floors in back and a perforated pink blanket, like somebody had poked holes in it with a pair of dull scissors. And it was my blanket and nobody could take it away from me. Even if they needed it more than I did."

———

"I'm going to keep your room just as you leave it," the old young man explained that night over dinner. He lit white candles in the mouths of dusty green wine bottles, and served lukewarm canned chicken broth in a pair of matching white ceramic bowls that had recently arrived in a Wal-Mart delivery van, along with a large oval-backed wicker chair, a gleaming palomino-white set of vinyl-covered luggage, a brand new sponge mop, and a plastic green pail. "It won't be like a shrine or anything. I won't allow it to get covered over with ribbons and rosaries and all that Mexican bullshit. And I'll only allow it to be visited by what I call genuine people, people with a permanent sense of the world. Some people, kid, never see the world for what it is. Some people just see themselves in everything, or government, or God. You say to them, hey, smell this flower, or feel the coolness in this rock, and they look at you like you're crazy. They suddenly remember all these important places they have to go, all these important things that need doing. Which, kid, as you probably know better than anybody, is just grade-A unadorned bull-puckey. There's only one place worth being in this stupid world, kid. And that's wherever it is that you already are."

The old young man had taken to wearing faded button-down long-sleeve shirts and thick gray over-washed dungarees with a brown leather belt. Sal didn't even think about him as the old young man anymore. He was suddenly stricken with youth, like somebody hit by a time warp.

———————

They came for her in a large empty school bus, with blue and green rainbows and shooting stars emblazoning the sides. The front hood was adorned with wobbly plastic eyes and a long, carrot-like plaster-of-Paris nose, and when Sal ascended the high leaning stairs, which were carpeted with a corrugated black plastic mat, she found herself in a long, cathedral-shaped chamber containing more than a dozen vinyl-covered black benches. Sal sat behind the driver, a gray-haired woman named Mal Granger who wore a blue Safety Zone uniform and black railroad-nail earrings. According to Mal Granger, she had raised several of her own babies when she was young, but then they grew up and moved away.

"Now I compensate for the loss of my babies by acting as a temporary mommy to all you beautiful, strange darlings who come along," she said, leaning forward to crank shut the pneumatic door with a long, subsiding hiss. "And I can't imagine a more satisfying job. Especially when it means acting as a savior to beautiful little girls like yourself."

It was the loudest transport vehicle Sal had ever experienced. It felt like traveling across incredible distances, even when the flat, dry scraggle-brushed plains crawled past. It was more like an approximation of velocity than velocity itself.

"What do you want to find when we arrive on the other side?" Mal Granger asked, her big eyes observing Sal from the flat rectangular spaces of the rear-view mirror, which hung on the inside of the windshield like one of those pop-ups on a computer screen. "I like to imagine who I'll be when I pass a place in the road – don't you? Like one moment I'm me, but as soon as I reach that dead tree up ahead then bing, I'll be somebody else. Are you looking forward to seeing your mommy and daddy again? Do you want to go to school, and make friends with other little boys and girls like yourself? What about a brand new bicycle, Sal? They received a shipment of brand new bicycles at the California Child Welfare Facility, and they're always looking for deserving little boys and girls to ride them. Do you want to be one of those lucky little boys and girls, Sal? Or is there something else you'd like to find waiting for you instead?"

The roads seemed to be getting wider, and the wider the roads grew, the more the bus seemed to inflate with the bus lady's expectations.

"I don't think I want a bicycle," Sal said after a while. Even the strange cacti and scrub-brushes were growing thicker and more prominent out here, like communities of knowledge. "I wouldn't know what to do with a bicycle if I had one."

Mal Granger rode high above the world in this big blue bus. She could travel back and forth across the same roads forever without ever having to step down from her torn vinyl seat. It wasn't fair, Sal thought. Some people had to live in the world, but some people didn't.

In the mirror, the disembodied smile grew huge. Rocky with gold crowns and silver-veined bridgework.

"Every little girl knows what to do with a bicycle," Mal Granger said, without turning around. "I'm no expert in child psychology, Sal, but even I know that."

THE LONG ROAD

She couldn't recall anything she might have missed. There were houses, of course, ensconced in their identical rectangular spaces. Trees and telephone poles, and birds who couldn't distinguish between them. Toys in the yards, and cars in the driveways, and leaves in the gutters, and sunlight on the rain-damp ceramic-tiled rooftops. And everywhere she turned, the sky met buildings at predictable angles, like patterns in a kaleidoscope. Dogs barked, cats twisted their tails atop fence posts, and pale white slugs pulsed underneath red ceramic pots and stepping stones. In the pre-noon stillness, the streets were uninhabited. But just because Sal couldn't see the people didn't mean they weren't there.

"There's nothing wrong with feeling a little strange at first. They live in that house, the one with the red front door and the blue-tiled walkway. They tried to have another child, but one thing led to another, and I don't know if they're even trying anymore. They haven't actually given up. They just need to achieve a little, well, not exactly closure. More like resolution. As in one chapter has come to an end, and another chapter's about to begin. You might be able to help, Sal. But don't worry about it. You're not under any obligation. You work out what you need to work out, and they'll work out what they need to work out. Just try to do it in the same house for a while, okay?"

It felt like driving with Mrs Mayhew, only they weren't going anywhere. Frank Morgan drove them around one block, and then around another. Some of the yards were bracketed with hedgerows. They reminded Sal of a board game with green squares and yellow pieces. A faint drizzle accumulated everywhere, imbuing the air with a grainy texture.

"I've been here before," Sal said softly, even though she knew she hadn't been — it just seemed like the polite thing to say. "In one of these houses, or one of these. That flowerbed, those yellow flowers. There were once two ladies with a green ottoman. Sometimes I slept on the green ottoman, and sometimes I slept between the two ladies on a small, lumpy mattress with too many blankets."

Sal realized she was whispering. She didn't want to provoke Frank Morgan into reaching for his briefcase and activating the flat gray tape machine. She didn't know if he could hear her or not. It probably didn't matter.

"Learning to love other people isn't what you'd call a piece of cake," Frank Morgan was saying. They were traveling up and down one small tree-lined street after another. "It just happens to be the way people are. If they don't form lasting bonds and kinship affiliations, they can't survive, and neither can their children. You either learn to adopt sympathetic behavioral strategies, and send Christmas cards, and go to mass, or you pass from the earth without a trace. So what do you say, kid? Should we go in and give it a try?"

They were slowing down in front of a house that had grown more familiar every time Sal saw it.

"Okay," Sal said. "Let's try."

Okay was an all-purpose word. It could be used in a wide variety of dissimilar situations. It didn't commit you to anything.

Frank Morgan "looked thoughtful" for a moment. He "knitted his brow." He "clucked his tongue." The air seemed to expire from deep inside him, as if he were suffering a slow air leak. For several moments, he formulated no expression whatever.

They were already parked at the curb.

"You don't have to go inside if you don't want to. I'll wait here as long as you like."

Sal wondered how long that might be.

That house over there.

And her in here.

———

It was as bad as she expected. There was a big room with wooden furniture and dark drapes, and, across the hall, a pink bedroom with pink drapes. Pink bedspread. Pink stuffed rabbits on bookshelves. Pink shoes in closets. The man and the woman followed her everywhere, but they never let themselves get too close, or too far away, as if they were herding a large billowy soap bubble. They were like babies – but with superficially adult abilities. They could walk. They could talk. They could go to work and pay bills. But their minds hadn't been fully formed yet. They couldn't seem to exist without Sal, as if she was the parent and they were the children.

"When a man and woman love each other," the woman explained, weeping softly into a succession of baby blue scented tissues, "they grow a baby in the mother's stomach until it's big enough to come out." The man and the woman were sitting across from Sal at a white formica table in a wide varnished kitchen gleaming with appliances and canned goods. "Then they give the baby a name, and decorate a bedroom for the baby, and as the baby develops a personality, they learn to love the baby even more. They live their entire lives for the baby, who eventually starts to look like, well, she starts to look like them. She turns into a little girl with her own personality, and her own sense of purpose. A little girl like you, Sal. A little girl with beautiful blonde hair and pink skin and, and, I'm sorry, I don't mean to be emotional. I promised myself I wouldn't be emotional but I can't seem to stop. Why does she keep looking at us that way?

Why can't I hold her? I can understand everything else, but I don't understand why I can't hold her."

The man was wearing a blue denim shirt and pale corduroy trousers. He sat close to the woman and hung his large left arm over her shoulder. With his large right hand, he held a mug of coffee. The mug was glazed ceramic blue, molded, organic-looking. The man held the mug almost as tenderly as he held the woman.

"Be patient, baby," the man said. Sal didn't know whether he was talking to her or to the woman. "We have to be patient. We have to consider what's best for her."

Sal looked out the brightly slatted Venetian blinds that shielded the kitchen window like high-tech armor. Through the angular segments of sunlight, she saw Frank Morgan sitting in his car at the curb, reading a magazine. Sal hoped it wasn't a very complicated magazine with too many words. Things around here were complicated enough.

The woman was tearing through Kleenex and clutching the soiled blue balls in her fists and under her arms. It was as if she needed to hold things that didn't matter: refuse, garbage, junk, Sal, whatever. Sal had never met a woman so frivolous in her affections. She didn't know how much more of this woman she could take.

The woman was looking directly at the man and the man was looking directly at Sal.

"When does she have to go? Can we fix her something to eat? Maybe we should show her the bedroom again."

"We're going to take our time and not rush things. Be supportive. Just like Mr Morgan said."

"I want to show her the pictures."

"You must not show her the pictures."

"Why can't I show her the pictures?"

The man was smiling faintly at Sal. It was the closest they had come to an understanding.

"Because the pictures are about who she *used* to be," the man said while the woman cried on his shoulder. "And what we need to teach her about is who we all are *now*."

———

Frank Morgan dropped her off every afternoon at lunch and returned a few hours later. Sometimes he sat in his car at the curb, or circled the block, listening to self-actualization tapes on his cd player, as if he were cruising the rim of a swimming pool, watching her watch him as she learned to tread water. Sal would watch cartoons with the woman, or help make dinner for the man when he returned home from work, dressed in a suit and tie and angry at everybody he worked with. Somewhere along the line, Frank Morgan stopped parking outside at the curb. Then he stopped coming back altogether. He never asked whether she wanted to stay. He just sort of took it for granted and left.

———

Some nights, the man and the woman brought folding chairs into Sal's bedroom and sat and watched Sal until she fell asleep in the pink bed. It made Sal wonder what they did with their free time before she came along to make their lives interesting.

"Would you like us to tell you a story?" the woman asked.

"I don't think so."

"Or sing you a song?"

"I don't like most songs. And the songs I do like, I can't remember."

The man and the woman didn't appear very comfortable. Sal couldn't understand why adults submitted themselves to bad chairs. Couldn't they find comfortable ones? What was the point of all that power if you didn't put it to good use finding comfortable ways of sitting?

Sometimes they lost interest in Sal's responses, and elicited random responses from one another.

"Should we tuck her in?"

"Maybe not yet."

"It might help her sleep."

"She sleeps fine. Why don't we just enjoy having her back and stop rushing things? I don't see what all this touching has to do with anything. When I get home from work, I just need to sit with my own thoughts for a while. I don't need to be constantly touching someone."

The man and the woman slept across the hall, where they shared a bath, shower, and toilet. They referred to their bathroom as the master bathroom; sometimes, without thinking about it, they referred to Sal's bathroom as the "guest bathroom," or the "pink bathroom," or the "one down the hall." After a while, it became a point of principle with Sal. She had no intention of using the "guest bathroom." She always insisted on using the master toilet instead.

"Is there enough toilet paper?" The woman was concerned about everything Sal did when she closed a door between them. "Are you sure you don't need any help?"

Sal liked the size of the master bathroom, and its warm varnished mahogany toilet seat. Sitting on the toilet seat with her underpants down and the woman on the other side of the door was about as good as this strange house got. Sal tried to take advantage of the experience as much as possible.

"I've done this before," Sal said calmly. "I don't see why I need help now."

The woman was always about to cry: Sal being too close or too far away, Sal in the bathroom or in the kitchen, Sal watching TV or looking out the window. It was like everything about Sal was painful and resistant and sad.

"I'm not trying to invade your privacy, honey. Please don't tell your father. You know how upset your father gets when he thinks I've invaded your privacy."

A painting of a green tree hung on one wall of the bathroom, like a window into another world. On another wall hung a small, framed, coaster-sized color photo of a very elderly man standing beside a very elderly woman in front of a white clapboard house. Sal was almost certain she had visited that house, and been welcomed by this same elderly man and elderly woman. She was just as certain that she shouldn't tell anybody about it.

The woman waited on the other side of the door. She was beginning to cry, softly, moistly, into some damp region of herself, like a deity of sadness. Sal couldn't bear to hear the woman crying so close to her. It spoiled the pleasure of being alone.

She wiped herself three times, even when she hadn't produced anything but the feeling of independence. Then she went back outside to watch the woman stop crying. The woman blew her nose. The woman couldn't seem to do anything without Sal's help.

"Well," the woman said sharply, clapping her hands together, as if she had just accomplished some private miracle. "How about we bake cookies, or chicken-fry a steak for your, you know, my husband. And then maybe we can watch some more cartoons on TV."

———————

Sal had never felt so entangled in other people's lives before: their dreams, their expectations, even their outlooks on life. It was as if Sal was learning she couldn't go away from people anymore. No matter how far away she went, they would find her. They would teach her. They would love her. They would tell her what to eat and what to wear.

"Is that you?" the voice said over the telephone. "I'd know your voice anywhere. Is that really you?"

Sal couldn't resist the telephone. It was the only thing she looked forward to anymore.

"Yes," she said, a little out of breath, standing alone in the wide house and feeling like a buried treasure without a map. "Of course it's me. Who else would it be?"

The woman followed from the kitchen, wiping her hands with a white towel. "Is that your father?" she asked. "If it's your father, I need to speak with him when you're finished."

Sal turned away from the woman. The woman had to understand that there were places she couldn't follow. She didn't need to worry, though. Sal would always be back.

"I thought so. I recognized your voice before you picked up the phone. You little bitch. You horrible vampirish blood-sucking little bitch. Saying those things about me, telling those lies. I know where you live, Stephanie, or Sally, or whatever you call yourself now, you little liar about everything, even your name. I can find you anytime I want. I have friends in the profession, colleagues who respect my professionalism. Despite all your horrible lies about my, my behavior. You little bitch. And when I get out of here, and get this fucking tag off my ankle so they can't pick me up on those fucking satellites, I'm going to come get you, I'm going to expose you for all those lies you told, and then I'm going to get my life back. I'm going to see to it that everybody finally learns who you really are, which is not the Redeemer of our Misfortunes, like I was originally fooled into believing, but the Purveyor of Darkness, the Dispenser of Suffering and Bad Faith. The Wretched Messiah. The Unholy Eater. The Believer in Nothing. I heard all those stories about you in my dreams, but I didn't listen. I was too mired in my vanity. I was too absorbed by my selfishness and greed."

Sal didn't know what to tell her. It was the problem with people. Once you knew them, you couldn't stop knowing them. And even if you could stop knowing them, they might never stop knowing you.

Finally, Sal said, "I'm sorry you feel that way, Mrs Mayhew. But now, if you don't mind, I have to go help the woman I live with. Tonight we're stir-frying chicken. I've never used a wok before. And there's no point putting it off any longer."

———

They attended noisy pizza restaurants, filled with clamorous game machines and pop music and children crawling through translucent plastic passageways like hamsters in mazes. They went to movies and parks and public sandboxes and playgrounds and swimming pools. The swimming pools were especially irksome, packed shoulder to shoulder with other children, everybody shrieking and splashing blue chlorine at everybody else. Sal stood in the middle of the wading pool and watched the man and the woman, who always stationed themselves several yards away.

"Try holding your head under water," the man said.

"Don't be afraid," the woman said. "It's only water."

Big children with plump red arms and thighs rocketed up from the surface, gleaming like seals and spouting blue streams. Huge inflated beach balls rolled past, aimlessly consistent, like sentient creatures. It was like enduring the slow surge and tumble of a washing machine, sudsy and inchoate, everything blending into everything else. Sal felt like a shell hurled onto the beach and taken back again, lifted and let down by tides other than her own. She couldn't understand why they made her stay in the shallow end. Why were they so worried and attentive? Water only made you clean.

During the day, the woman would sit with Sal at the kitchen table and encourage her to complete art projects. She provided pots of paste, and plastic-wrapped sets of colored pencils, and sheets of colored paper and crayons and felt-tipped pens and scissors. Then she sat across the table and looked at Sal, as if she were about to say something important.

"I don't feel like drawing," Sal said. "I wouldn't know what to draw even if I wanted to."

The woman's face had grown dry and flaky, especially around the eyes and nose. It was as if the tears had drained her face of flexibility. She was growing old and used up.

"It doesn't have to be anything specific," the woman said. "It doesn't have to be a picture of something you've seen. Just draw anything that pleases you. Colors, maybe. Or shapes. If you're embarrassed, we won't hang them on the wall. We'll throw them in the trash and you won't have to see them again."

Sal felt a chill run down her spine. She thought of the bicycle in the garage, with a padded pink seat and pink tassels on the handlebars. The woman wasn't looking at Sal. She didn't need to. For the first time since Sal came to live here, the woman possessed weight and dimension. She wasn't just this aimless somebody waiting for the man to come home and tell her to stop crying. She was a person. She was making Sal her guest.

"Before you went away I taught art in elementary school," the woman said, picking at a flake of skin beside her left nostril. It was clearly the least important thing the woman had ever heard herself say. "I've seen so many kids' drawings, I won't even look twice at yours. If you prefer, I won't even sit here. I'll go into the next room and watch TV."

For several days, Sal drew pictures on the slippery formica table, without pleasure or remorse, scratching out figures and shadows of figures with a sort of benign clockwork regularity, like typing numbers onto a computer screen. And the woman never once told her what to do or how to do it. She only made the sort of enquiries that any sensible person would make when confronted by the sorts of pictures that somebody like Sal drew.

"What's that?"

"A road."

"And where's it going?"

"Nowhere. It's going past that town."

"And what's in that town?"

"People. And houses with yards."

"Are they nice people?"

"I don't know. I haven't drawn them yet."

"Are they mean people? Do they do mean things to you?"

"Most people are pretty nice. But you can't see them — they can only see you. They aren't walking on the same roads as you are. They live in these houses, and these are their lights. And these are the windows where they watch you pass by."

"What's this?"

"A road going in this direction. And another road going in that one."

"This?"

"A sign."

"What's the sign telling you?"

Sal thought for a moment. She had seen lots of signs. She couldn't be sure if she was remembering a specific one, or inventing a composite of all the signs she had ever known.

"It says carry on down this road. Or carry on down that one. They're both the same in the long run. Nothing bad will ever happen to you. You'll find your way home in the end."

———

She drew pictures of people with beards, people with bald heads, people with wings, people with flaming bodies, people with dogs on leashes, and people driving down the road in weirdly-shaped automobiles, trying to find their way to the store and back again. She drew pictures of swingsets and slides, and the full moon staring down from mountaintops, and waves on a beach, and trees in a desert. She drew pictures of a coyote with an orange tail, and a washing machine with a round window, and a dry, flat landscape broken by fissures and large jagged cracks. She drew pictures of two little girls walking over a mountain. She drew pictures of one little girl waving goodbye from the back of a car.

"Who's this little girl?"

"My sister."

"What's her name?"

"I can't remember. She may not have said."

"What would you tell her if you saw her again? Would you be glad to see her? Would she be glad to see you?"

Sal found it easy to draw things. But it was much harder explaining what they meant.

"I guess I'd tell her what you always tell little girls. That everything's going to be okay. Don't worry about a thing. Your daddy will be home soon."

***

Something was coming towards Sal, but nobody could tell Sal what it was, or how soon it would get here. It was like awakening on a dark road in the middle of the night and hearing an engine in the distance. They were coming. They knew where they were going, and you knew where you were going, and if you maintained your mutual trajectories long enough, you would meet, bound by the same conditions, liable to no thoughts but your own. Then, just as suddenly, they would be gone again, and you would be standing on another road, staring in a different direction. Another engine in the distance. Another intention in the night.

"Please wait here," explained Mrs Abrams. "I'll be right back. There are magazines, puzzles, and even a board game or two. If there's a problem, push that red buzzer on the desk. As you'll notice, there's another little girl in the room you can play with. I'll leave you both to get on with things as you wish."

Sal regarded the little blonde girl on the sofa from far away, as if she were looking through a pair of inverted binoculars. The little girl didn't look up. She was trying to fit a rolled-up magazine into her mouth. The magazine was smudged all over with chocolate and raspberry sauce.

"Of course I trust you," Sal said, to nobody in particular. "But even if I didn't, I'd still feel safe in this room."

It was not a large room. You couldn't live here. It possessed one large mirror and no windows. Perhaps Mrs Mayhew was behind the mirror, or even Grandma. That would be an example of what adults referred to as "turning the tables." That would be an interesting trick to play on somebody as well-organized as Mrs Mayhew.

The little girl was aimlessly kicking her legs and examining her knees. She wore a blue dress. Her hair was long and smelled nice, making Sal feel lonely and inadequate. I don't think I ever once wiped her face with a damp rag, Sal thought. And now look at her. Blonde and tidy and prettier than me.

"Don't look up," Sal said softly, sitting down beside her on the sofa. She erected a hard mental pane of distance between them. "Don't let on you know me. Just pretend that I'm not here."

The little girl didn't seem to be listening. She was being either very attentive, or very inattentive – Sal couldn't be sure.

Sal sat silently with her hands folded in her lap for several minutes. Time seemed to matter again. It always mattered most when it was going away.

"We never finished our book," Sal whispered softly, "and now it's too late." If a stranger was walking by the room, it would appear as if she were speaking to herself. "Everything I've seen and done, and all the people who knew me – they only matter to you now. I'm sorry if I ever seemed selfish or self-involved. I only wanted somebody to remember me, and know who I really am and how I really feel, but I know that's not important anymore, it's actually sort of impossible really. So please forget everything I told you. Pretend like we never met. You don't need to remember me anymore because I'll always remember you, and all the places we saw together, and all the things Daddy did for us. After all, it was never us that mattered. The only person who ever mattered was Daddy."

———————

"I loved you with the best I had in me," Sal could hear Daddy telling her as she gazed out her bedroom window into the hard glare of the night. "But sometimes, honey, our best isn't good enough. We're too weak to love the people we care about. We run out of steam. Mainly, we lack the courage and conviction to love somebody without remission. Better to feel no love at all, we decide. Rather than suffer this too-sad love we can't control."

By the time the moon rose, the man and the woman had usually turned off all the lights and gone to their bedroom across the hall. Even if Daddy finds me again, Sal thought, he won't be able to get inside the house as easily as the first time. The first time, he was invited. The woman fixed him coffee. She even paid cash in advance, though he never looked once at the boiler.

He just took one look at Sal and that was it.

"Sometimes we wake in the night with the conviction that this isn't our real body," Daddy liked to say, especially when he was sitting on the edge of Sal's bed watching her fall asleep. "We itch in all the wrong places; we feel compressed and uncomfortable. Our clothes don't fit, even stuff we've been wearing for years. We begin to suspect that our actual bodies are in another house entirely, watching TV with the sound off, or mowing the lawn. Maybe we're eating pizza or baking bread, or maybe we're taking night classes at the high school. But whatever we're doing, we know that this isn't the *real* us lying here, talking to this strange person beside us. It's the same way with families, Sal. We find ourselves alone in strange houses filled with strange people. We know their names and what they do for a living. All their documents are in order. But deep inside our skin, we don't belong with them. We're already somewhere else. We're just pretending to occupy this house until our real lives come along."

———————

At night, if she sat quietly, she could see across the hall into the master bedroom. Sometimes the man and woman moved slowly together, darkness passing across them like eddies from another world. Then they moved quicker. Then they stopped. They might remain quiet for a while, but eventually they began to speak softly, discussing things they had discussed before.

"Is she awake?"

"I don't hear anything."

"She seems happier. Doesn't she seem happier to you?"

"She seems the same."

"She's definitely happier. She likes doing art at the kitchen table. She doesn't seem so sad, especially when she's eating. She answers the telephone. She takes part in everyday activities."

"She used to be excited to see me. Especially if I brought her things from the store."

"And she stopped making those noises. You know the ones I mean. When she's standing at the window and sees cars go by."

"Now, when I bring her things, she just looks at them. Turns them one way, then the other, and puts them down again. Like those Buffy Top Trumps the other day. The guys at work say their girls all love the Buffy Top Trumps, but she hasn't even opened hers. I must have given her the Buffy Top Trumps as long ago as last week."

Sal decided her room was darker than their room. That was why she could see them and they couldn't see her.

"What about the doors, honey? Did you lock all the doors?"

"Don't start, Amy."

"Especially the basement. Every time I turn away for a second, she's down in the basement. In that little space under the front stairs, with the moldy sacks of concrete and the mousetraps. Sitting there and making that noise. And I wonder sometimes, honey, if that's really our little girl in there. Maybe they brought us somebody else. Somebody who looks like our daughter but who isn't her at all."

Sal felt sorry for them. But not any sorrier than she did for everybody else.

"I forget if I asked you or not. Did you lock the doors? Especially the basement."

"I locked all the doors. Especially the basement."

"What about the garage?"

"It's on the remote deal. You can't open the garage without the remote."

"There are two latches on the garage door. One on each side."

"The garage door is fine. If somebody opened the garage door, we'd hear them a mile away. Please go to sleep, honey. I don't know how much longer I can keep going over this. I'm being as patient as I can."

———

One night, Sal dreamed of all the people going away, chained together at the ankles by flashing infra-red monitoring scanners and bar-coded identity tags. Their baggy gray one-piece uniforms were cinched around their waists by thick white ropes; their heads were shaved down to the nub. Men and women of various sizes and dimensions; working class people and white-collar people and uniformed people employed by the government. Even the people Sal had recently met were there –

Officer Fortinhue and Judge Betty and Frank Morgan and all the concerned care-givers at California Family Shelters – shuffling along in their leather sandals and loose-fitting cotton shirts, too ashamed to look up as they filed past in awkward little swerves and counter-swerves, like the segmented body-parts of some gigantic centipede. "They've all done bad things and now they're going away," somebody said. "Showed you too much attention or not enough. Touched you in the wrong places or not at all. We can't let them be in our world anymore, so we're sending them somewhere else." The man's voice was both familiar and unfamiliar, just the way Sal liked it.

When Sal awoke in her dark bed, she was sweating, as if somebody had poured a pitcher of warm water down the front of her dress. Her underpants were drenched, and the moisture made thick squelching noises on the plastic under-sheet when she sat up. Sal pulled back the blankets and peeled off her pajamas. She didn't believe in wetting the bed. Wetting the bed was something little girls did when nobody cared about them, and here was Sal, in her bed, who everybody cared about. Even the people she had never met.

There were no cars on the street when Sal let herself out through the garden gate.

You travel as far as you can and you see as much as you can and when it's over, Sal thought, it's like you never saw anything or went anywhere at all. At this time of night, the only lights that appeared in houses were activated by small plastic timers connected to wall sockets and lamp cords, humming like absence, completely artificial and pre-planned.

Sal could see her own breath in the air, emerging from her lungs in moist droppletted bursts of herself. Her footsteps carried her on a thin cushion of sound. She wasn't an individual anymore; she was an emanation of someone else. She walked past blue mailboxes, brown telephone poles, yellow hydrants, blue mailboxes again. White laser-printed notices for lost dogs and children, husbands and wives who hadn't come home, cars and mopeds for sale, block parties and garage sales and book groups and political action committees. It was like walking on a circular loop around the same points on the same grid. It was the sort of progress that made Sal feel hopeful and alone.

You heard the world before you saw it. It happened every time. The rush of cars on distant freeways, and then the shuddering emergence of sound, the internal thrum and whisper of basic, elemental matter. Sal didn't even turn around when it approached, blowing ropes of exhaust from its rattly undercarriage.

"Hey there, little girl," the man said. "What're you doing out here all alone, a little girl like you, so late at night without her mommy and daddy to take care of her. Do you want a ride, little girl? Maybe I could take you somewhere. Maybe I could look after you until your proper mommy and daddy come back from wherever it is they've gone. What do you say to that, little girl? You wanta get into my car and keep me company? Maybe we could sing songs, or go to a movie. Do you like movies, little girl? I'm a big fan of movies myself."

He was talking at her through the passenger window as he drove slowly beside her, as slowly as Sal walked, contorting his body and shoulders until he fit the frame, almost as if he were trying to crawl out of the car while driving it. He wasn't like Daddy at all. Daddy never talked to Sal when she was outside the car. He only talked when she was inside with him.

"No, thank you," Sal told him. She felt reassured by the continued slap of her sandals on pavement. Suburban houses stood solidly in every direction. Nobody who lived in these houses would let anything bad happen to Sal. They knew it and Sal knew it. They would simply observe Sal's progress through the world until she was gone.

"Pretty little girls don't grow on trees," the man said. He was leaning his forehead against the inside of the windshield, the dashboard littered with crumpled cigarette packs, improperly folded road maps, sticky paper clips, and parchment-like credit card receipts. "When people find beautiful little girls, they need to look after them. They need to teach them decent behavior, and warn them about the sort of people who aren't so nice as they are. If you get into my car, little girl, we could drive somewhere special, like an ice cream parlor, or maybe Disneyland. Have you ever been to Disneyland, little girl? It's a long trip, but you always get there faster than you think."

It was the part about life that would never change and never go away. People everywhere, standing at all the windows, filling up cars and freeways and buses, flying around on jumbo passenger planes, and visiting Disneyland and ice cream parlors and pizza palaces and movie theaters and coming home again to fondly recall where they had been. People of every shape and size and description, good people and bad people and all the people in between. Everywhere Sal went she would find them already looking for her. They would take her home. They would feed her and bathe her and send her away the next morning. People who wanted to love Sal but not any more than they had to. Because when you got right down to their basic essential stuff, people were all exactly the same. They had all been written down in the same book that Sal would never read.

———

When Sal returned to the house, they were asleep in the big bed, lying on their backs, propped up by pillows in an attitude of benign inattention, incognizant of the sounds Sal made as she entered their bedroom and observed the configuration of objects that defined their spaces and made them real. The thick blue drapes with lacy borders. The large wooden bureau with burnished brass handles. The blue pitcher of tepid water on an end table beside the bed, and two clear plastic cups, and the radio alarm clock, and the stuffed pink elephant with buttons for eyes, and a string of sewn-on glitter for a mouth. It made Sal sad to realize that this stuffed pink elephant was the most interesting object in the room. It was certainly the only thing worth talking to.

"I went as far as I could," Sal whispered, "and came back again. I almost wrote a book, had the same Daddy twice, slept on a baseball field, and presided over flooded basements and dead cars. I learned the names of a thousand people and forgot them just as fast. I sent people to prison for treating me improperly, and slept in a Laundromat, and almost got married. And then, when I least expected it, they brought me here through a state-operated child-protection program, and told me I belonged here, and that I couldn't leave until I was so old that I didn't have anywhere else to go. My full name is Salome Erin Jensen, but I think of myself as Sal. Sal who went away and came back. Sal who draws pictures on the kitchen table. Sal who sleeps in a small bed and isn't as affectionate as she should be. Sal who made the world hers until it didn't want her anymore. I realize that's a pretty complicated thought to share this late at night, but it's something I had to say and now I'm done."

THE DROP EDGE OF YONDER
A NOVEL BY RUDOLPH WURLITZER
A Trade Paperback Original; 978-0-9763895-5-2; $15.00 US

* *Time Out New York*'s Best Book of 2008.
* *ForeWord* Magazine 2008 Gold Medal in
  Literary Fiction.

"A picaresque American *Book of the Dead*... in the tradition of Thomas Pynchon, Joseph Heller, Kurt Vonnegut, and Terry Southern." —*Los Angeles Times*

1940
A NOVEL BY JAY NEUGEBOREN
A Trade Paperback Original; 978-0-9763895-6-9; $15.00 US

"Intelligent and absorbing . . . subtle and affecting."
—Tova Reich, *Washington Post*

"Taut, nuanced, beautifully written." —*Commonweal*

SOME THINGS THAT MEANT THE WORLD TO ME
A NOVEL BY JOSHUA MOHR
A Trade Paperback Original; 978-0-9820151-1-7; $15.50 US

* *Oprah Magazine* Top 10 Terrific Read of 2009.
* *The Nervous Breakdown* Best Book of 2009.
* *San Francisco Chronicle* Bestseller.

"Mohr's first novel is biting and heartbreaking... it's as touching as it is shocking." —*Publishers Weekly* (Starred)

I SMILE BACK
A NOVEL BY AMY KOPPELMAN
A Trade Paperback Original; 978-0-9763895-9-0; $15.00 US

"Powerful. Koppelman's instincts help her navigate these choppy waters with inventiveness and integrity."
—Paul Kolsby, *Los Angeles Times*

THE CAVE MAN
A NOVEL BY XIAODA XIAO

A Trade Paperback Original; 978-0-9820151-3-1; $15.50 US
* *WOSU* (an NPR member station) Favorite Book of 2009.

"As a parable of modern China, [*The Cave Man*] is chilling." —*Boston Globe*

EROTOMANIA: A ROMANCE
A NOVEL BY FRANCIS LEVY

A Trade Paperback Original; 978-0-9763895-7-6; $14.00 US
* *Queerty* Top 10 Book of 2008.
* *Inland Empire Weekly* Standout Book of 2008.

"Miller, Lawrence, and Genet stop by like proud ancestors." —*Village Voice*

CRUST
A NOVEL BY LAWRENCE SHAINBERG

A Trade Paperback Original; 978-0-9763895-8-3; $15.00 US

"A postmodern examination of the self that teases the very idea of postmodernism... that rare bit of lampoonery that is both humorous and smart."
—*Los Angeles Times*

THE SHANGHAI GESTURE
A NOVEL BY GARY INDIANA

A Trade Paperback Original; 978-0-9820151-0-0; $15.50 US

"An uproarious, confounding, turbocharged fantasia that manages, alongside all its imaginative bravura, to hold up to our globalized epoch the fun-house mirror it deserves." —*Bookforum*